WE RIDE FOR CIRCLE 6

The danger-prone drifters truly believed the small Circle 6 spread would become their sanctuary, a safe resting place after so many years of outlaw-fighting and knight-errantry. How wrong can a couple of trouble-shooters be? Even before they stowed their gear in the bunkhouse, Circle 6 became the powder-keg of Loomis County. Soon enough, Larry & Stretch were up to their ears in mayhem, intrigue and gun-trouble.

MARSHALL GROVER

WE RIDE FOR CIRCLE 6

A Larry & Stretch Western

Complete and Unabridged

LINFORD
Leicester

First Linford Edition
published 1996
by arrangement with
Horwitz Publications Pty
Australia

British Library CIP Data

Grover, Marshall
    We ride for Circle 6.—Large print ed.—
Linford western library
1. Australian fiction—20th century
I. Title II. Series
823 [F]

ISBN 0-7089-7877-0

Published by
F. A. Thorpe (Publishing) Ltd.
Anstey, Leicestershire

Set by Words & Graphics Ltd.
Anstey, Leicestershire
Printed and bound in Great Britain by
T. J. Press (Padstow) Ltd., Padstow, Cornwall

This book is printed on acid-free paper

1

The Big Dry

ONCE in a while he felt the need to get away from his ranch, his wife and daughters, his foreman and his few hired hands. This morning was one of those rare occasions for Dabney Frecker, boss of the Circle 6 spread of Loomis County, Nebraska. He had quit Sun Basin right after breakfast with the idea of hunting jackrabbit in the open terrain between the basin and the route to the county seat.

Dab never did get to shooting that morning. He gave up on his hunting plans when he spotted the tall strangers and their challengers, four rough waddies of Diamond H, biggest cattle outfit in the whole territory.

By the bank of sluggish Farley Creek,

Dab squatted on a flat rock with his rifle resting on his knees and raised his eyes to the timber ridge above. The tall strangers were crossing, moving stirrup-to-stirrup, when the four Diamond H riders appeared at its other end and signaled them impatiently. Having passed the half-way mark, the strangers kept coming.

"You deaf, saddlebum?" one of the ranch-hands bellowed. "I said back up! Make way for us!"

A few yards from the east end of the bridge, the strangers reined up. It was a narrow structure, this bridge, only intended for horsemen. Riders crossing the creek at this point could go across Indian file or two abreast, but never bunched. Dab Frecker now heard one of the newcomers address the proddy quartet; his voice was deep, penetrating and mild right now; he was appealing to reason.

"Easier for you boys to clear your end and let us through. We're almost across anyway. Backin' clear to the west side don't make much sense."

"Damn it, we're Diamond H!" snapped another waddy.

"You don't back-talk Diamond H men," warned one of his cohorts. "What we say goes, savvy?"

The other stranger now appealed to the bumptious Diamond H men, and Dab noted his accent was similar to his companion's. He knew that drawl. These were Texans. Tow-haired and homely with his lantern jaw and jughandle ears, this wayfarer grinned a guileless grin and suggested,

"It don't seem reasonable to wrangle thisaway, fellers."

"We feel like wranglin'!" retorted the burlier of the four. "Now are you backin' up — or do we toss you in what's left of the creek?" He invited them to inspect the discouraged-looking stream spanned by the bridge. It was early spring and the temperature unseasonably high. Rain hadn't fallen in this region since the beginning of winter and now Loomis County was in the grip of drought. "Not much water down there — but plenty mud."

"I noticed," said the dark-haired Texan.

"You backin' up — or do we have to get rough with you?"

"Well, we ain't backin' up."

"So you're askin' for it!"

★ ★ ★

Every detail of that short fracas was followed with eager interest by a 50-year-old rancher of slight physique, placid disposition and gregarious instincts. Dab Frecker prided himself he could get along with all his fellow-men, the exception being Kyle Hammond, boss of Diamond H and employer of the four waddies now attacking the Texans.

As soon as the four dismounted and charged at them, the dark-haired man swung down, revealing himself to be all of 6 feet 3 inches tall and uncommonly brawny. His friend stayed astride his pinto pony, but did not exclude himself from the mayhem. The first man to reach the dark-haired stranger aimed a blow, missed and was seized and flipped over the rail to pitch into the creek. The second and third made a vain attempt to drag the other Texan from his mount, only to suffer similar treatment. One was grasped by an arm and hauled up and over and, during his wild-yelling, ungraceful descent to the muddy stream, his companion got between the sorrel and the pinto and began clambering up with the idea of straddling the pinto, the better to pummel its homely rider. Somehow, that strategy just didn't pay off. The taller Texan leaned down, gripped him by collar of jacket and back of pants-belt and, with no apparent effort, whisked him off his feet and up and over. He too hurtled to the mud.

The fourth waddy launched a savage attack on the dark-haired stranger, landing two hard blows which didn't seem to have any effect. He suffered prompt retaliation, a nose-bloodying jab that dazed him. Again, Dab Frecker was profoundly impressed; the dark-haired man used only one hand to raise and toss his assailant over the rail. Four irate aggressors now sprawled in the clinging mud of Farley Creek, heaping curses on the strangers, gasping threats.

"You bastards better keep movin'!"

"Get your butts clear outa Loomis County!"

"You ain't gettin' away with this!"

"Next time — we'll pay you off — but good!"

The dark-haired man remounted. As the strangers finished their crossing to the east side, Dab retreated to his horse, returned his rifle to the saddle-sheath and climbed astride. He caught up with the tall riders when they had travelled only another 50 yards east.

"Hold on there, boys. Like to talk to you." As they reined up to look him over, he identified himself. "Dabney Frecker's the name. I own a spread hereabouts. Circle 6 is my brand."

"Howdy," nodded the dark-haired man. "I'm Valentine. My partner here is Emerson. If you're friendly, I'm Larry and he's Stretch."

"I'm friendly," Dab assured them with an approving grin. "In all of Loomis County, you ain't apt to meet a friendlier citizen. Except maybe Tim Doherty."

"Doherty a rancher too?" enquired Larry Valentine.

"Nope," said Dab. "Tends his own bar in Loomis City."

"Don't that sound good?" Stretch Emerson heaved a mighty sigh. "Runt, don't you wish we were tellin' Doherty howdy right now, hookin' our boots on his brass rail, wrapping our paws round the handle of a tall jug o' beer?"

"I'm so damn dry," complained Larry, "I could strike a match on my tongue."

"If you boy's crave to 'tend your thirst, I'm buyin'," offered Dab. "But you'll never make Loomis headed this way. This track leads back to my place.

You lookin' for the county seat?"

"Any town'll do," said Larry.

"I know a few short-cuts," said Dab. "If you're acceptin' my invite, I could get us to town . . . " He fished out an ancient Horologe and squinted at it, "in less'n an hour."

"Best offer we've had in many a long week, runt," remarked the taller Texan.

"You always this sociable with strangers?" Larry asked.

He was studying a veteran who, out of his saddle, probably stood 5½ feet or so, a man whose eyes did not shift from his intent scrutiny and whose stubbled visage appealed to him. Nevertheless, hard experience had taught him to be cautious.

"Well, I'm a fair judge of men," shrugged the Circle 6 boss. "And I particularly admire the way you handled them Diamond H bullies."

"Saw that foolery, did you?" prodded Stretch.

"From down by the creek-bank,"

8

nodded Dab. "When I quit my place this mornin', I was hankerin' to down a couple cottontails. At my age a man ought to keep his shootin' eye sharp. Didn't spot no critters. Just you buckin' them proddy waddies. Glad I saw it. Did my old heart good. Listen, I figure I'm as thirsty as you. Do I ride to town alone?"

"I reckon not, Mister Frecker," Larry decided with a genial grin. "So lead on."

"My bunkhouse gang calls me 'Mister'," said Dab, as they started for the county seat. "My ramrod, old Orv, he calls me Dab. Take it kindly if you boys do likewise."

During the journey to Loomis, he scrutinized his tall companions and threw out a question or two. They were even more impressive at close quarters, formidable despite their nonchalant demeanor. Larry of the dark thatch and ruggedly-handsome features showed a generous width of shoulders and chest but no thickness about the midriff. His range clothes had seen better days. He was well-mounted and armed; the sorrel looked to have power and speed and, in addition to the .45 holstered at his right hip, the stock of a Winchester jutted from his saddle-scabbard.

Packrolls, saddlebags and sheathed Winchesters completed the effect, confirming these two to be the wandering kind, nomads whose animals toted all their wordly possessions.

Stretch he guessed to be somewhat more easy-going than his partner, a gangling beanpole whose buscadero-style shell-belt was equipped with an extra holster at his left side.

"One handgun ain't enough?" Dab asked.

"Balance," quipped Stretch. "I'm clumsier'n Larry. He can pack one Colt and walk straight. Me, I'm apt to keel over."

"Don't mean to pry," Dab assured them later, when they reached the regular trail to the county seat. "You're welcome to invite me to mind my own blame business, but I'm askin' how long you've been on the drift."

"Longer'n we can recall, Dab," drawled Stretch. "And I guess we don't mind you askin'."

"But we work too," Larry pointed out. "Handled all kinds of chores in our time."

"Bein' Texans, I'm bettin' you've mostly worked cattle," said Dab.

"Safe bet," shrugged Larry.

"You'd be from the Panhandle country," Dab supposed.

"And that ain't exactly sheep country," grinned Stretch.

"So you've seen a drought or two," opined Dab.

"A drought is bad medicine," muttered Larry.

"Ain't that the truth," agreed Stretch.

"This territory's been too long without rain," Dab told them. "Scarce a drop fell early winter. And, after that, *nary* a drop. Now it's almost spring and feelin' like midsummer already,

11

wells quittin', waterholes dryin' up. You saw how Farley Creek looked. Be cattle dyin' pretty damn soon, and I'm gettin' to feelin' guilty."

"Why guilty?" demanded Larry. "A drought ain't any man's fault."

"If you could see Circle 6, you'd know what I mean," said Dab. "My herd's feedin' on sweet graze. I own every acre of Sun Basin and, all year round, we got water. All we need. Spring half-way up the north slope. Flows clear across the basin floor to my south quarter where it dams up good. The lake, we call it."

"So you got water and the other ranchers ain't," shrugged Larry. "Rough on 'em, but you can't blame yourself."

"There's only one other spread," Dab told him. "The big spread — Diamond H. Used to be three other outfits, good neighbours of mine. Kyle Hammond bought 'em out, took over their range on account of he's runnin' better'n six thousand head. That's a lot of beef, so he sure needed all that extra land. Mind now, I ain't sayin' he ran 'em off. The way I hear, it was all legal, every rancher collectin' a fair price from Hammond."

He said nothing more until they reached the county seat, as sizeable a cattle town as the Texans had seen in a year of drifting. They rode four blocks of its broad and dusty main street to dismount in front of one of Dab's favorite retreats, looped their reins and trudged into that small bar to listen approvingly to their host's next words, four words of infinite appeal to them.

"Set 'em up, Tim."

Jovial and portly, bald save for the grizzled red hair at his temples, Doherty had three tall beers set on the bar by the time they reached it.

"Top o' the mornin' to you, Dab. The wife and daughters?"

"Givin' me no more trouble than I deserve," smiled Dab. "Tim, meet a couple friendly strangers, Larry and Stretch."

The Texans shook hands with

Doherty, sampled preliminary gulps of cold beer, hooked heels on the brass rail and dug out Durham sacks. While they rolled and lit cigarettes, Dab filled his bent-stemmed brier, got it drawing to his satisfaction and continued to talk cattle and drought, that tragedy dreaded by cattlemen the world over.

In the middle of this discourse, he muttered a question that caused his tall guests to frown into their beer.

"You boys ever get weary of driftin' all the time?"

They traded glances. Larry nodded and assured Dab, "Sometimes, yeah. We get plenty weary of it."

And that was an understatement. Time and time again, during their nomadic wanderings, these fiddlefoots had cursed their fate. They considered themselves to be hexed and they had their reasons. Looking for trouble was not their style, or so they claimed. Since quitting the Lone Star State at the end of the war, they had sought an elusive Utopia, a piece of territory unmarred by violence, enmities, outlaw activity, a tranquil place providing good hunting and fishing for men craving the lazy life. In the war, as Confederate cavalrymen, they had done more than their share of fighting.

They had fought even harder and had suffered more from '65 till now. The lawless had become their natural enemies. Try as they might, they could never turn a deaf ear to the plea of an oppressed homesteader or any other kind of pioneer, any law-abiding citizen in any kind of danger. Their altruism had plunged them into one violent battle after another and, to the delight of frontier journalists, to the chagrin of the lawless and sometimes the resentment of law officers, they had survived those battles. They had never sought trouble, upheaval, tension, the threat of sudden death, but the hex continued to dog their trail.

Somehow, Stretch's amiable disposition and carefree outlook had survived. Larry's sense of humour was not entirely defunct. It surfaced now and then, despite the cynicism he had shown in recent times.

"Like to make you an offer," said Dab. "If you can work cattle as slick as you handled them proddy fools at the bridge, I can sure use you. How long since you nighthawked, worked a round-up, helped drive a pay-herd to a railhead?"

"Quite a time," Larry said softly.

"But we ain't forgot how," declared Stretch. "Some things a man don't forget — ever."

"You don't want to be tied down — I already guessed that," said Dab. "But, listen, I wouldn't try to hold you to Circle 6 for the rest of your lives. I'm short-handed right now, know what I mean? So maybe you'd relish a little bunkhouse-livin', ranch chores, just till we got my beeves rounded up and delivered to Omaha. I pay regular. Forty and found. You ain't apt to wrangle with the other hands and you'll get along fine with Orv, my foreman.

As for Roscoe the cook — well — who ever heard of a sweet-tempered cook? Circle 6 is a right friendly spread and you'd be mighty welcome."

Larry grinned wryly as he enquired,

"Hammond riders been crowdin' you — the way they tried to bulldog us at the ridge?"

"What do you care?" countered Dab. "You already proved you can handle that bunch."

The drifters finished their beer. Larry dropped a coin on the bar and watched Doherty draw refills.

"What's your feelin'?" he asked Stretch.

"All spring," mused Stretch. "Ranch grub. Ranch chores. Sharin' a bunk-house again. We keep busy, maybe our feet won't itch."

"Bunkhouse beats a trail camp any time," opined Larry.

"And the pay's regular," said Dab.

"Ain't the pay that matters, Dab," said Stretch. "We got — how much, runt?"

"About two hundred and seventy between us," said Larry. Automatically, he began assuring the rancher, "We came by it honest. Might seem like a fat bankroll for a couple fiddlefoots, but . . ."

"You don't have to convince me you ain't crooked," Dab said gruffly. "Told you I'm a fair judge of men. So there's my offer. You want time to think on it?"

"Listen now, runt," frowned Stretch. "Workin' cattle can't buy us the kind of trouble we run into while we're on the drift. Dab's spread got to be a safe place for us."

"And spring won't last forever," nodded Larry.

"Let's do it," urged Stretch.

"All right, Dab," said Larry. "Seems like you just got yourself a couple new hands."

"You'll do fine," Dab confidently predicted. "So what do you say? You want to hang around, look the town over, or ride on back to the spread with me? I'm ready to go."

"The longer we hang around this burg," warned Stretch, "the better our chances of gettin' prodded into another ruckus."

"Damn right," agreed Larry. "So okay. We put this beer where it belongs and stay with Dab."

It happened that Doherty's Bar was located directly opposite the stagecoach depot. Neither Texan showed any interest in that building when, a short time later, they quit the bar with the Circle 6 boss. And Dab would not have spared the depot a glance had the tall man on the driver's seat of the stalled surrey ignored him. However, Kyle Hammond, owner of Diamond H, sighted Dab and at once called to him.

"Frecker! I want a word with you!"

It wasn't a request. It was a demand, a brusque summons. The Texans paused to eye Dab expectantly and to appraise the man on the surrey seat. Hammond was lean, handsome in his well-tailored town suit topped off by a planter's hat, a dark-haired, impressive man. Larry guessed him to be in his mid-30's. And, right now, he was beckoning Dab. Impatiently.

"Over here, Frecker!"

Stretch asked quietly, "Who's the big shot?"

"Hammond — couldn't you guess?" Dab stood by his horse, frowning in Hammond's direction as he muttered an order to his new hands. "Ride to the north end of town and wait for me. I'll be with you in a little while."

While slipping their reins and preparing to mount, the Texans scanned the immediate vicinity. A few locals, the inquisitive type, were pausing to covertly study the oddly contrasted ranchers, the one so authoritative, so demanding of respect, the other so slight of physique, self-effacing, almost nondescript. Was Hammond alone, or were there Diamond H hands in town, waddies as proddy as the four encountered at Farley Creek?

They swung astride and started their horses moving slowly northward, alert for their first glimpse of a Hammond rider, a potential trouble-maker.

Dab waited for the Texans to move out of earshot before calling a rejoinder.

"You want to talk to me?"

"Right now!" scowled Hammond.

"So here I am," shrugged Dab. He tapped dottle from his pipe, pocketed it and lounged against the hitch-rail. "You want it private, or do we holler at each other across Main Street?"

Hammond swore under his breath as the onlookers traded nervous glances. In Loomis, no man dared defy the county's most influential citizen. People deferred to him, made way for him and were careful not to offend. And here was Dab Frecker showing no deference, refusing to budge.

Colouring angrily, Hammond dropped from the surrey and started for Doherty's hitchrail. Dab maintained his non-chalant posture and, when confronted by the handsome 6-footer, showed no fear, just mild curiosity.

"You did that deliberately, Frecker," Hammond quietly accused. "It's come to that, has it? You'd publicly humiliate me?"

"Young feller, I don't aim to humiliate myself." Dab kept his voice as low as Hammond's. "And that's what I'd be doin' if I jumped to your whipcrack, if I went scuttlin' across to you any time you holler at me."

"Now see here . . . " began Hammond.

"I'm just a small rancher," said Dab. "To the likes of you, Circle 6 seems like just a two-bit outfit. You're bigger'n me, better educated and plenty rich. But that don't mean you can order me to your fine surrey like you'd summon one of your hired hands, savvy?"

"Well . . . " shrugged Hammond.

"There are many years between us," Dab pointed out. "You're supposed to respect age — or didn't you know that?"

"Damn and blast!" breathed Hammond. "You have the nerve to reprimand me? What're you fishing for — an apology?"

"I don't need no apology," said Dab. "Now, if you got somethin' to say, I'm listenin'."

"I've said it before, old man," muttered Hammond. "You know what's on my mind. Farley Creek is mostly mud, the Loop Wash isn't much better and my waterholes are starting to dry up. I need water for Diamond H stock and I'm not begging for it. Sun Basin . . . "

"Is Circle 6," Dab reminded him. "I own it all."

"True enough," growled Hammond. "So I'm repeating my offer. And you have to admit it's fair. Why, you'd leave Loomis County a rich man!"

"I'm rich enough right now, son," drawled Dab. "Livin' on land that's mine, raisin' prime beef and makin' no trouble for my neighbors. I don't send my hands out night-raidin'. Can you say that for Diamond H?"

"Drought sets an edge to tempers," Hammond said defensively. "Only natural my men can't be restrained, Frecker. You're hogging all that Sun Basin water — and they're seeing Diamond H stock thirsting, ready to drop."

"So they work off their spite on Circle 6 hands," accused Dab. "I used to have seven. Your bully-boys kept leanin' on 'em, fazin' 'em, beatin' up on 'em till they couldn't take it no more. Four of my best hands up and quit. I ain't complained to Sheriff Tarren, and you know why. I've seen him tip his hat to you many a time. But heed this, young feller. Next time it happens, I'll be swearin' charges against Diamond H."

"It doesn't have to be this way, Frecker," frowned Hammond. He glanced southward, grimacing impatiently. "The stage is due. I'm here to meet my sister and her fiance. She got engaged while visiting our aunt in

24

Omaha. Listen now, Frecker, I can't waste any more time arguing with you, so I'll boost my offer — by another thousand. You have to admit that's more than generous."

"Certainly is," agreed Dab. "And I'd grab at it — if I hankered to sell out and quit."

"You could make a fresh start in Wyoming, California, anywhere," said Hammond. "Some area far from this damn drought."

"Somethin' you just don't savvy, son," said Dab. "Circle 6 is my homeplace. I built it, paid for that basin with the savin's of a lifetime, Addy's and mine. You don't just walk away from somethin' that took so long to build — and I sure as hell ain't."

"You're a stubborn old idiot!" snapped Hammond.

"Plenty stubborn," nodded Dab. "But no idiot. You ever take me for a fool, you'll be in worse trouble than me."

"Be it on your own head from here

on," Hammond said bitterly. "You're not asking for trouble. You're *begging* for it!"

"Some day you'll understand — maybe," sighed Dab. "That day your men drove Diamond H steers into the basin was your mistake, not mine. Nobody talked to me. Nobody asked. Your ramrod and a half-dozen of your hands started runnin' a couple hundred head down my south slope — just as if Sun Basin was part of Diamond H range — so I had my men turn 'em back."

"Frecker, I don't beg!" warned Hammond.

"Have it your way," shrugged Dab. He slipped his rein and raised boot to stirrup. "'Scuse me. Got to be gettin' back to the spread now."

"I'm not through talking!" raged Hammond, as Dab swung astride.

"I am," retorted Dab.

With that, he nudged his mount to movement and began riding north along Main, leaving the Diamond H boss to curse in impotent fury. Aware all eyes were on him, Hammond made the effort to regain control of himself. He lit a cigar before strolling across to the depot.

Larry remarked, while riding out of town with his new boss, "It don't look like a dried out town, this Loomis. Not yet anyway."

"Guess it's just a matter of time, huh?" asked Stretch.

"Everybody prayin' for rain," Dab said moodily. "Wells in town're still givin' water. But on all the land hereabouts, right where it counts most, the only good water's in Sun Basin."

"How d'you feel about Diamond H waterin' their stock in the basin?" asked Stretch.

"*Wouldn't* have minded," declared Dab. "All Kyle Hammond had to do was ask. Not beg. Just ask. I'd have obliged. But he's got to be so big since he bought out the other ranchers — maybe too big for his britches.

He ain't askin'. He's demandin'. And that makes a heap of difference." He sighed heavily and challenged the tall men riders flanking him. "You bucks're thinkin' I'm just a stubborn old coot."

"No," said Larry, eyeing him sidelong. "More to it. You're kind of like us, Dab. Ain't nobody gonna push you around — right?"

"Right," nodded Dab. "If I backed down from Kyle Hammond, I'd never feel the same. I wouldn't be my own man. Nobody's gonna take *that* away from me." He was silent for the next quarter-mile. Then he confided, "I got two good reasons why I won't sell out to Hammond. He made me a fair offer, sure. Better'n fair. But Circle 6 is home to us Freckers and that's where we're stayin'."

"I call that a good enough reason, Dab," said Larry.

"The other reason is, if I sold out, Hammond would own every acre of graze in this county," said Dab. "Already, he owns everything except

Sun Basin, and I figure that's plenty. To me, it just don't seem right for one man to own so much, his brand on every critter. It'd make him kind of like a king hereabouts. Wouldn't be the mayor runs the town nor the sheriff runnin' law enforcement. It'd be Kyle Hammond. Everything'd be Kyle Hammond. No . . . " He shook his head emphatically, "I liked it better when there were four or five spreads in Loomis County. Man such as Hammond starts wantin' it all, well now, that's just got to mean trouble."

"Like you say, he's gettin' too big for his britches," opined Stretch.

"Enjoys bein' boss — enjoys it too much," complained Dab. "I don't believe he's all bad. Not deep down. His sister now. Miss Anna. Puny little thing and a real lady. He's been lookin' out for her since their folks died, and that was a long time back. She's some younger'n him, so I guess he's more'n big brother. Kind of like a father to her. Treats her real gentle, I hear tell. Nothin' but the best for Miss Anna. Proves he ain't all bad, huh?"

"I guess," shrugged Larry. He let his gaze move over the browning landscape of the terrain ahead. The change was all too evident, green showing only in small patches. Unless the heavens opened within the next 6 or 7 weeks, the land hereabouts, including every sprawling acre of Diamond H range, would become a dustbowl. "Everybody prayin' for rain, huh Dab? Well, maybe the Lord'll oblige."

"That's faith," said Dab. "You can afford faith, Larry. By early summer, you and Stretch'll be long gone from here."

Kyle Hammond had not resumed his perch on the front seat of the territory's most admired surrey. On the porch of the stage depot, he paced restlessly, pausing only to check his watch and call impatient questions to the depot-boss and the ticket clerk. Always the same answer. No, the westbound was on schedule. Barring mishaps, it would arrive at 11.10, not a minute before or after.

At 11 a.m., Hammond's foreman and a trio of cowhands, the escort party, emerged from a saloon a few doors away and came along to join him.

"Too hot for spring," remarked the foreman. Ed Rushford was a 6-footer and burly, broad-faced and flatnosed, his dark mane close-cropped. "After Durango Bend, the stage-trail'll be plenty dusty. Mighty uncomfortable for your guest, him bein' an easterner."

"Let's remember he *is* a guest, this Mister Dortweil." Hammond made sure his hired hands heeded this warning. "He'd have to be a gentleman. No other kind could court a woman like my sister."

"Well, that's a fact, Mister Hammond," one of the hands said respectfully. "Miss Anna bein' a lady and all."

"You passed the word?" Hammond

challenged Rushford.

"Every man on the payroll been told," nodded Rushford. "Won't be no foolery tried on Mister Dortweil. He feels like ridin', no smart-aleck'll saddle a half-broke horse for him."

"No rough stuff, no practical jokes," stressed Hammond. "Anna will be mighty sensitive about it. Maybe she'll end up married to Dortweil and maybe not. She hasn't known him all that long and she's not a woman to be hustled into anything. But I want them — both of them — to have every chance."

"And you'll be wantin' to size him up," guessed Rushford.

"You'd better believe it," Hammond said fervently. He cocked an ear, checked his watch again and stared beyond the buildings on the east side of town. "I see moving dust. Stage'll be here soon."

On to Loomis rolled the westbound, carrying the slender young woman who, since her early teens, had aroused her brother's protective instincts. Anna Hammond was coming home and bringing a guest, the man who had won her heart and, already, Kyle Hammond was apprehensive.

2

Like Old Times

FOUR of the six passengers remained seated after the stage stalled in front of the depot, approving the handsome easterner's eagerness to alight first and assist Miss Anna Hammond from the vehicle. Well-groomed and urbane, his blond hair neatly barbered, Howard Dortweil cut an impressive figure as he descended and nodded to his host.

"You'll be Kyle of course. I recognize you from Anna's description. Could we postpone the exchange of greetings till I've helped Anna down?" Without waiting for an answer, he turned back to the coach door, doffed his derby and extended a hand. The auburn-haired, demurely gowned Anna leaned out to trade smiles with her brother and allowed her suitor to assist her from the vehicle and onto the porch, there to be embraced by her kinsman.

"There, Kyle," Dortweil said jovially. "Safe delivery of the precious lady."

Released by his beloved sister, Hammond held her at arm's length for an intent inspection.

"Fragile as ever," he frowned.

"But feeling well, Kyle," she happily assured him. "And excited!"

"Excitement isn't good for you," he muttered. "Sis, it does my eyes a treat, seeing you again."

"I missed you too," she murmured. "And now I want you to start getting acquainted with Howard."

Brother and guest shook hands and traded amiable smiles. Very much the solicitous host, Hammond expressed the hope the stage journey had been reasonably comfortable. Dortweil declared he had enjoyed every moment of it and looked forward to his stay at Diamond H.

"An extended stay, I hope," said

35

Hammond. "Let's say for an indefinite period, Howard."

"Most generous of you, Kyle my friend," beamed Dortweil.

"I was sure you two would take to each other," smiled Anna. She caught sight of an old friend advancing toward them, and chuckled indulgently. "Oh, my! This really completes the welcoming committee."

"Thunderation." Hammond followed her glance and good-humoredly warned Rushford and the other men, "Stand clear — give her room. If there's a collision, you'll be knocked clear to the middle of Main Street."

"Kyle, that's cruel," Anna protested, but she was still laughing.

The fat woman was of an age with Anna Hammond. She was now Mrs. Harper McQueen, wife of a local alderman, a cheerful, double-chinned young woman of ample proportions, unashamedly obese, unfailingly cheerful. From Loomis, in earlier years, Anna and Dorrie had travelled east together to finish their education; they had remained firm friends ever since.

"Better late than never!" beamed Dorrie. "Welcome home, Anna. And how was Omaha and your dear aunt?"

While Anna introduced the courtly Dortweil to the sizeable Dorrie McQueen, Rushford and the ranch-hands transferred baggage from the coach to the rear of the surrey. Extra items were secured to a spare horse and, by then, the fat woman was remembering it was near feeding time for her younger child. After hugging Anna again, she hurried away.

"Time to go, Anna," urged Hammond. "You'll have ample time for your unpacking after lunch. Also some much-needed rest. You're looking pale again."

"Just a little travel-weary," shrugged Anna, as Dortweil helped her into the surrey.

This morning, three newcomers to Loomis County were reacting to the local scene in different ways.

Out at Circle 6, the Texans were anticipating they would very soon settle in, at least for the spring. Sun Basin was indeed a lush oasis in this drought-stricken territory, its green-carpeted floor attracting them from the moment they reached the south rim with Dab and began the descent. From the spring half-way up the north slope, just as Dab had described it, the basin was irrigated by a steady-flowing stream that became, below and to their left, the lake. Sleek Circle 6 steers watered there and grazed on almost every section of the flatland. Some distance from the lake stood the double-storied ranch-house, the barn, cook-shack and bunkhouse, log and clap-board structures, strictly ultilitarian. The usual network of corrals, some trees providing shade, ample water, ample good graze — Circle 6 had it all.

"But, some of these days, I'm maybe gonna burn off all the brush and chaparral up the east and west slopes," growled Dab. "The hell of it is — it'll grow again in no time at all. See them two young fellers over to the west side? They're flushin' strays. Have to do it all the time. Cattle're plenty dumb, right? Got good graze and water on the bottom land, so what do they do? Keep climbin' up them east and west slopes to get their horns tangled and their hides scratched in the brush."

"Looks to be maybe a dozen head strayed up there," observed Stretch.

"That's Fat Pat and Elroy huntin' 'em out — makin' hard work of it as usual," said Dab.

"Tell you what," offered Larry. "Now that we're on the payroll, how about we ride over there and lend a hand?"

"Yeah, you do that," nodded Dab, "while I go ahead and tell Roscoe to dish up for two extra hands."

The arrival of the tall strangers took the stray-hunters by surprise. Immersed in their irritating task, they flushed three steers out of a tangle of brush and, when they began fazing them down the slope, caught their first sight of the newcomers pushing the other nine. A few more minutes and the four riders were descending abreast, the bunch-quitters several yards ahead.

"Howdy there." The taller Texan nodded affably. "We're a couple new hands. He's Larry, I'm Stretch."

Fat Pat Barnes and Elroy Hagenthorpe were, they discovered, somewhat grumpy and dispirited for their tender years, neither of them more than 23. Pat Barnes was around 5 feet 8 and deserving of his nickname, a roly-poly waddy. Elroy was taller, lean and worried-looking.

"Could've done a heap better for yourselves," he mumbled.

"Don't look that way to us," drawled Larry. "Seems like a right fine spread, Circle 6."

"Right unpopular spread," growled Fat Pat. "Diamond H hates our guts. Before you know it, Hammond's hard cases'll be givin' you a bad time, and then Circle 6 won't seem like such a fine spread to ride for."

"Only three of us," said Elroy. "Five, if you and your buddy stay on. Five — against the whole Diamond H bunch. Damn it, there's better'n a couple dozen of 'em."

"And all of 'em mean," fretted Fat Pat. "And plenty tough."

Over lunch in the bunkhouse, the new hands were sized up by Dab's foreman, the rangy, slow-moving, solemn-visaged Orv Moran. Having reached his 50th year, Orv Moran considered himself to be past his prime and far over the hill. He was, in fact, savoring his status of elder cattleman, developing a complex — and willingly. The thatch was iron-grey, the droopy mustache a perfect match and the demeanor reminiscent of the hundred and one old timers Larry and Stretch had seen whittling, warming their arthritic bones in the sunshine of many a frontier town, usually occupying seats outside barber-shops or livery stables. Yes, Orv was

41

working it for all it was worth, the right to slow down in deference to his years.

"A fool tells himself he's as spry as he ever was," he intoned, while munching on his meat. "A wise man accepts." He pointed a gravy-smeared knife at the new men. "That's what counts, see? Acceptin'. I'm old and I know it and I don't mind if I got to slow down. A man's gotta grow old, so he ought to do it with dignity. You savvy what I mean?"

"Well, sure," nodded Larry, who secretly hoped he would be as healthy at the ramrod's age. "You're makin' good sense — I guess."

The other Circle 6 men were not without their hang-ups, as the Texans soon realized. Fat Pat and Elroy seemed to spend most of their waking hours in dire dread of further attacks from Diamond H. Their colleague, Shorty Rudge, shared this fear and also cultivated a king-sized complex about his height. He was a chunky young fellow who stood 5 feet 5 inches, but seemed runtier because of his barrel-chested physique.

"Got his lovin' eye on one of the boss's daughters," Fat Pat informed the new hands. "The younger one, Lucy Lou. That's because she's some shorter'n him, makes him feel real tall." He grinned unsympathetically. "Just as if he was full-growed."

"I'd sooner be short than lard-bellied," retorted Shorty.

"No hard words while I'm eatin'," chided the ramrod. "At my age, I gotta digest my grub careful. Stay cool, you young'uns."

"Who can stay cool?" grouched Elroy. "This is a helluva way to live, never knowin' when them Hammond jaspers gonna faze us again."

"Hammond riders can be licked," Orv assured him.

"No they can't neither," muttered Fat Pat. "They're the toughest, the roughest . . . "

"Four of 'em got their come-uppance

this mornin'," announced Orv, switching his gaze to the Texans again. "Dab told me about your little run-in. At your age, I'd of done likewise. Different nowadays, now that I'm too old for such shenanigans."

"Hey? What run-in?" demanded Shorty.

"It was nothin'," shrugged Stretch. He attempted to change the subject by calling a compliment to the cook. Roscoe Cully, balding, pot-bellied and surly, was trudging around the seated hands collecting used dishes. "Hey, Roscoe. Fine chow. You're some helluva cook."

Roscoe jerked to a halt, frowning suspiciously.

"You smart-talkin' me, tall boy?"

"He means it, and so do I," Larry assured him. "Fine chow, Roscoe."

"You can keep Roscoe's grub on your stomach," grinned Fat Pat, "just so long as he don't spike it with his rotgut."

"Don't call it rotgut!" raged Roscoe.

"That ain't rotgut I'm distillin' in my secret place. Some day, when I get it just right, I'll be juggin' the best whiskey any drinkin' man ever tasted. The day will come! Mark my words!"

He stamped out, after which Larry dropped his voice and appealed earnestly to the ramrod.

"You better explain to us about Roscoe and his secret place and all. We're new here. We'd like to get friendly with the whole outfit."

"Hard to get friendly with them you can't savvy," Stretch pointed out. "So help us savvy Roscoe."

"He's crazy," sneered Elroy.

"Got a bee in his bonnet and a chip on his shoulder," declared Shorty.

"Even so, he's got his reasons," muttered Orv. "There's always a reason for the way a man is."

"So how about Roscoe?" asked Larry.

"Worked for one of them big distilleries back east, the Cronin company, till he got himself fired and

45

come west," Orv told them. "The way it seems to me, he was mixin' a little of this and that into the steeps and the mash tuns, figurin' he could improve the booze. Convinced himself he knew better'n them that paid his wages."

"Mighty lucky they caught him at it," opined Fat Pat.

"Damn right," nodded Elroy. "He might've poisoned every whiskey-drinker in Illinois."

"They kicked him out," Orv went on. "And, ever since, he totes this grudge against saloonkeepers and all the big liquor companies. Still claims he's gonna come up with — uh — what he calls the perfect blend — a masterpiece — or some such craziness." He offered an assurance. "All you got to remember, if you crave to keep your health, is don't ever bust into Roscoe's secret place, meanin' his still. That's the shack back of his kitchen. Stay out of there and don't ever drink any of his moonshine — not one little bitty sip."

"Blow the top of your head right

off," warned Fat Pat.

The new men hoped the other subject was forgotten, but Shorty proved them wrong.

"What run-in?" he demanded of Orv.

"These two." The ramrod gestured to the Texans. "Boss-man spotted 'em crossin' the bridge at Farley Creek." He went on to repeat Dab's account of that brief set-to and, with a bland grin, remarked, "Kind of proves somethin'. Ain't a man can't be beat."

The reactions of their new colleagues both intrigued and saddened the veteran trouble-shooters. There was no elation except for a short-lived burst of enthusiasm from Shorty, whose grin faded and died when Fat Pat soberly opined.

"They got lucky is all. Ain't natural for just two men to whup double their number in Diamond H waddies."

"Why'd it have to happen?" complained Elroy. "Hell! They been humiliated. That'll make 'em meaner now. Next Circle 6 man they get their hands on, they'll beat the daylights out of him. And, with my luck, it's just bound to be me!"

The cook had returned in time to hear Orv's report. His reaction was different again.

"Huh! Them Diamond H bucks. You want to know why a couple Johnny-come-latelies could get the better of four of 'em? I'll tell you why. Only booze they drink is that swill from the saloons in town. There just ain't no decent liquor sold anyplace. They've been drinkin' saloon-bought booze and it's picklin' their gizzards and slowin' 'em down." He stared hard at the Texans. "If you was sober when you tangled with 'em . . . "

"Oh, sure," nodded Stretch. "We was real sober."

"So," shrugged Roscoe. "That was an easy chore for you. They were weak-muscled from saloon booze — an easy victory I call it. Couple ten-year-old kids could've licked them, the shape they were in."

"You're probably right, Roscoe," said Larry.

"I wish you hadn't of done that to 'em," sighed Elroy.

"Wasn't nothin' else we could do, amigo," frowned Stretch.

"'Cept back our animals clear back to the other side of the creek," drawled Larry. "Which would've been plain foolish."

"But safer for all of us," mumbled Fat Pat. "Now you've gone and made 'em madder."

Somehow, the Texans managed to conceal their feelings. Dab's bunkhouse gang was some dispirited, well and truly intimidated bunch, and that was an understatement. No fire. No get-up-and-go. This saddened them, though they conceded these young men were just working stiffs after all; the warrior instinct did not surface in every bunkhouse on the frontier and all ranch-hands weren't necessarily fast and accurate with a gun or able to hold their own in a fist-fight. Dime novelists back east were creating a myth and, as it happened, the much-travelled drifters were leery of myths. Nevertheless, they regretted the chronic shortage of morale at Circle 6.

The meal ended, the ramrod high-signed the new hands to follow him outside. Lounging by a corral-post, he announced the next essential of the settling-in ritual of this spread.

"You have to meet the family now, Dab's wife and daughters. Mind now, that don't mean you get invited into the house. Dab'll fetch 'em out to the porch. Don't reckon I have to warn you jaspers about mindin' your manners."

"We'll be real polite," promised Stretch.

"Bachelor myself," remarked Orv. "Bein' past my prime, I sure ain't matrimonially inclined. How about you?"

"Bachelors," Larry said firmly.

"Since the day we was born," declared Stretch. "And we aim to stay that way."

"So you won't be gettin' ideas about Miss Desdemona or Lucy Lou," nodded Orv. "Well, that's kind of fortunate. Me now, I ain't about to bet who them purty gals is gonna end up wed to. Shorty's been makin' eyes at Lucy Lou, but she won't give him the time of day. Desdemona gets her man-hungry heart to flutterin' every time she sights Deputy Symes, but he acts like he don't know she's alive. It's the other deputy, Toddy Allsop, that's tryin' to court Desdemona, only she don't encourage him none. As for Symes, only female he cares about is Sheba Gilliam that runs the Jezebel Saloon in town."

Having filled the Texans in on matters that did not concern them, he escorted them away from the corrals and across to the ranch-house. They were ordered to stand in the yard a respectful distance from the porch and wait. Orv then ventured into the house to reappear a few moments later and gesture them to readiness. They did what was expected of them, baring their heads and holding their battered Stetsons to their chests as Dab escorted his womenfolk out to the porch.

His spouse, Addy, was a plump lady whose demeanor caused the drifters no alarm. However, the avid appraisal of willowy Desdemona and her trim-figured sister started them flinching.

"Aren't they *tall* . . . ?" enthused Desdemona.

"And so handsome!" twittered Lucy Lou. "Papa, are they single?"

"Lands sakes!" sniffed their mother.

"Hold your hosses," Dab chided his daughters. "Why in tarnation did I spend good money to have you girls educated right? Act ladylike, for pity's sakes. You ain't even introduced yet. Addy honey, our new hands. Taller one's called Stretch. Other one . . . " He grinned amiably at Larry, "I guess he'd only be six, three or thereabouts. He's Larry."

"I'm sure you'll be reliable," murmured Addy.

"Right kind of you to say so, ma'am," nodded Larry. "We aim to do our best."

"Desdemona and Lucy Lou," offered Dab, indicating his off-spring.

"Our pleasure, ladies," said Larry.

"Well, heavens, you don't have to be so formal," smiled Desdemona.

"Yes they do," countered Addy. "They're hired hands and the kind who know their place."

"That's the pure truth, ma'am," Stretch assured her.

"I'm twenty-one and I can cook the kind of food that melts in a good man's mouth," bragged Lucy Lou.

"I make all my own clothes," announced Desdemona. She fluttered her eyelids at Larry and added, "I'm sweet-natured too."

"Disgraceful!" gasped Addy.

"I reckon that'll do," growled Dab. "Addy, take 'em back inside." He grimaced in exasperation. "Durned if I savvy why they strain at the bit. Ain't as if they're thirty-five."

"Young and purty and with plenty time ahead of 'em," commented the ramrod. "Kids nowadays. Always hustlin'." As Addy Frecker began shooing her daughters into the house, he predicted, "When you get to be old — like me — you'll know better than to rush anything."

Freed of feminine distraction, Dab advanced to the top step and squatted there to fill his pipe.

"You got any special chores for 'em, Orv?" he asked.

"They could ride the slopes," Orv suggested. "Check all the chaparral and the brush, kind of scout the whole spread, get used to the place."

"Do that," Dab urged the Texans. "Got your own horses stabled snug? Fine. Choose yourself a couple from the string and start gettin' the feel of the outfit." He drawled another question to his ramrod, "You gonna put 'em to night-hawkin'?"

"Tomorrow night'll be soon enough," said Orv. "Shorty's turn tonight."

"Somebody rides sentry every night?" prodded Larry.

"We ain't had trouble every night," shrugged Orv. "But there's been a raid or two. No cattle run off. Just Hammond riders tryin' to spook our boys."

"Herd's well fed and watered," Dab pointed out. "Ain't yet stampeded, but we can't take chances. You makin' out all right with the rest of the outfit?"

"Just fine" nodded Larry.

"Orv warn you about Roscoe's still?" asked Dab.

"Sure, and you don't have to worry," grinned Larry.

"We ain't about to steal none of Roscoe's moonshine," declared Stretch.

"That ain't what I mean," said Dab. "I don't want anything bad to happen to you boys and I'm always afeared Roscoe's still gonna blow up one of these days. I can always hire another cook, but good cattle-hands ain't all that plentiful in this territory."

"Don't smoke in spittin' distance

of that damn shack of Roscoe's," counselled Orv.

"We'll remember," promised Larry.

From the corral housing the string, under the watchful eye of the ramrod, the new hands selected a charcoal and a roan and led them to the barn for saddling. En route, they passed a corral in which just one animal, a wild-eyed calico colt, prowled and stamped and snorted unsociably.

"Don't never get close to Whitey," warned Orv. "Ain't full broke yet. Wasn't nobody could finish the job."

"Until he's broke, he ain't earnin' his feed," said Larry.

"You'll get your chance if you like livin' dangerously," shrugged Orv. "But time enough later."

Soon afterwards, riding patrol of the brushy and timbered slopes of Sun Basin, the veterans traded comments and mutually agreed they were glad to be here. Trips to the county seat would be few and far between, and this suited their purpose. As Stretch put it,

"In a town — and specially in a saloon — we most always get prodded into a ruckus. Out here is safer. Ain't likely we'll ever lock horns with them young'uns, Fat Pat, Elroy, Shorty."

"Ain't likely they'll lock horns with *any* man," opined Larry.

"Not exactly bright-eyed and bushy-tailed, are they?" sighed Stretch.

"Not so you'd notice," said Larry. "Diamond H got 'em good and buffaloed."

"Ain't that the truth," Stretch lamented. "I swear I never saw three healthy young bucks so spooked."

"Can't blame 'em, I guess," shrugged Larry. "They're the kind signs on to work cattle, not to get prodded and bullied and shot at."

"But it's sad, huh?" frowned the taller Texan.

"Mighty sad," said Larry. "They don't know it, but a spark of courage, a little fire in their blood, would make 'em easier of mind. They'd be a whole lot happier."

"The hell of it is young'uns is hard to teach," said Stretch. "Won't listen to the likes of us. So it just ain't no use us tryin' to tell 'em anything."

"Will you quit talkin' that way?" grouched Larry. "Consarn you, we ain't two old timers workin' with kids."

"Maybe so" said Stretch. "But they're some younger'n us."

"Some younger," Larry conceded. "But old enough to show a little spunk — 'stead of backin' down to Diamond H."

After their first circuit of Sun Basin, it was clear to them that Dab Frecker's analysis of the current situation was accurate. Diamond H had attempted no peaceful negotiation at the start of the big dry. Had Hammond done so, Dab would have dealt fairly with him, there would have been no ill feeling and no feuding.

"Which makes this Hammond a stiff-necked fool too proddy for his own good," was how Larry summed it up.

Lunching in the expensively furnished

dining room of the Diamond H ranch-house with his sister and guest, Kyle Hammond was not now behaving as a stiff-necked, proddy fool. He was impressed, almost over-awed in fact, by his guest's poise and aplomb, his casual dissertations on the share market, on stocks and bonds and the international financial scene. Howard Dortweil was Hammond's idea of the typical successful stockbroker, warranting his respect. And so he strove to be the gracious host.

While the men talked, Anna Hammond was content to listen approvingly, making no attempt to join in the conversation, her gentle smile reflecting her pleasure that her brother and suitor, the two most important men in her life, now socialized so easily.

Dortweil good-humoredly chided himself for monopolizing the conversation and began questioning Hammond about the prevailing crisis in this territory.

"As I understand it, you're facing a difficult situation, Kyle."

"Difficult enough," nodded Hammond. "The biggest herd ever seen in these parts, and desperately in need of water. Diamond H won't fail, however. There's an obstacle, but I have my own way of overcoming obstacles."

Anna nervously interjected at that point.

"A range war is not the answer, surely. To me, it seems tragic, this bad feeling between you and Mister Frecker."

"What do women know of business?" Hammond appealed to his guest.

"Very little," smiled Dortweil. "And that's as it should be. Women, especially a lady of Anna's quality, should be protected from such matters."

"If you really meant what you said — about exploring Diamond H land — you won't see it all in an afternoon," warned Hammond. "We're big, Howard. As big a cattle outfit as you'd ever find in the state of Nebraska."

"But this is Anna's home environment,"

60

said Dortweil, eyeing her fondly. "She was born and raised here, and that makes Diamond H very important to me. To know her better, I should get to know the land." He nodded to his host again. "On the other hand, I can hardly expect you to give me the guided tour, Kyle. You're obviously far too busy."

"You're that eager to take a ride this afternoon?" asked Hammond. "I'll say this for you, Howard. The stage journey didn't tire you."

"I feel the urge to be out and about on a good mount," said Dortweil. "Kyle, I have a suggestion. You have much to discuss with Anna, she having been away two months or more. So, while you two are catching up, I could change to riding clothes and — here's an idea — how about that foreman of yours? If he can spare an hour or two, perhaps he could be my guide?"

"Ed Rushford," nodded Hammond.

"Seems a reliable fellow," remarked Dortweil.

"Don't know how I'd manage without him," said Hammond. "He arrived, he and five friends of his, right when my need was greatest. That was about eighteen months ago. My old foreman couldn't be dissuaded from taking off for California. He had gold fever — an incurable case, I'm afraid."

"Dear old Mister Brennan," Anna said reminiscently. "He always seemed the typical cattleman, didn't he? Men do change."

"The change was sudden and dramatic," Hammond told his guest. "Brennan's brother was a prospector, an amateur at that. Imagine the luck. He'd been fossicking only a couple of weeks in the Sierra Mateo when he struck the richest pay-vein ever seen in that territory and staked his claim. Of course he wrote to my foreman, urging him to become his partner."

"And that was the last we saw of Pete Brennan," said Anna.

"Fortunate that this Rushford fellow

arrived at so opportune a time," said Dortweil.

"Well, Ed was an experienced ram-rod," shrugged Hammond. "I had a bunkhouse full of reliable hands, but none of them had what it takes to make a good ranch foreman." He finished his coffee and traded glances with his sister. "You're right, Howard. I'd appreciate a private get-together, just Anna and me."

"It's settled then?" asked Dortweil. "You can arrange it with your foreman?"

"Be glad to," nodded Hammond. "Right after lunch."

Some 20 minutes later, with his sister beside him he stood at the window of the upstairs parlor and watched Dortweil, now attired in more serviceable garb, ride east from the ranch headquarters with Rushford as his escort.

"He rides well," he observed. "Quite a man, little sister. Fine manners and good background, obviously a gentleman."

"And well to do," she murmured, as they withdrew from the window and seated themselves. "So, after we're married, you'll not need to worry about me. I'll be well provided for. Oh, Kyle, I'm so looking forward to my first sight of Howard's fine home in Wisconsin. Now tell me . . . " She smiled eagerly. "What do you think of him? Isn't he handsome — And so impressive?"

He lit a cigar and surveyed her intently.

"Anna, what *you* think of him is what counts. You've known him less than two months. I'm not saying that's a bad thing. I just want you to be very sure of your feelings."

"I'm grasping at straws, is that what you mean?" she sadly challenged.

"We have to be sensible about this, and cautious," he pointed out. "He's your first suitor, Sis. Over the years, the eligible bachelors of this territory haven't worn a path between Diamond H and the county seat. If that sounds brutal, I'm sorry, but . . . "

"No, you're quite right," she shrugged. "I've never been the kind to turn men's heads, to win admirers."

"So give it time, that's all I ask," he muttered. "It's not that I'm questioning Howard's sincerity. It's just — seeing you together . . . "

"You wonder what he sees in me," she accused.

"And that *is* brutal," he sighed. "Fine thing for a brother to say. You're the last woman whose feelings I'd want to hurt."

"You're just being your reliable, practical self," she said. "I'm not offended, Kyle. Your protective instinct is my greatest security."

"There are other considerations," he suggested. "Your health, for instance. You're still — well — delicate. I'm sure the Omaha visit was beneficial but, to me, you don't seem any stronger."

"I feel quite well," she assured him. "Not as energetic as other women perhaps, but . . . "

"That's putting it mild," he fretted.

"You tire too easily. And that reminds me. Loomis has a third doctor. Hung up his shingle a few days before you left for Omaha. Solemn young fellow name of Jansen who keeps pretty much to himself, but old Doc Conrad and Reverend Pickard speak highly of him."

"And you think I should consult this new doctor?" she frowned.

"Not rightaway," said Hammond. "But, next time you have one of your fainting spells, why don't we have him out here to check you over? As I hear it, he graduated from medical school only a year ago. It's quite a time since Doc Conrad first came to Loomis, twenty years or more. Must've been a lot of new discoveries in medical science in recent times, new techniques, new treatments. So — why not?"

"Whatever you say, Kyle," she nodded. "I must admit it does become irritating at times — being so listless. But do we need to mention this to Howard? I don't want him to think he's courting a weakling, a semi-invalid."

"Not a word to Howard," he said reassuringly. "It's a family matter anyway."

Once out of sight of the handsome double-storied Hammond home, Dortweil and his companion slowed their mounts to a walk. Rushford accepted a Havana cigar, lit it and grinned sardonically.

"Big spread, huh?"

"Massive," said Dortweil.

"This drought won't last forever," drawled Rushford. "Diamond H is a bonanza, pal. Richest spread I ever saw. And it's gonna be ours."

"Exit Kyle Hammond," muttered Dortweil. "Enter the new owner of Diamond H."

3

The Predators

WHEN Dortweil complained of the rising temperature, the Diamond H ramrod guided him to a shaded grove. There, they rested their animals and squatted side by side on a lightning-blighted log to trade questions and answers.

"You're sure she'll inherit?" demanded Dortweil. "We can't afford to overlook anything, Ed. The possibility, for instance, of some forgotten relative showing up after Hammond's death."

"It's for sure," shrugged Rushford. "The girl is Hammond's only — what do you call it . . . ?"

"Beneficiary."

"That's it. The old gal in Omaha, their aunt, got her own fortune."

"But how reliable is your information?

Remember now, we're playing for high stakes."

"How's *this* for reliable? The night this Griffin feller was out to the spread for supper, him and Hammond took the air on the porch after the girl turned in. She always turns in early. Kind of puny. You've noticed, huh?"

"I know all I need to know about the girl. Tell me about Griffin."

"He's a lawyer in Loomis, been lawyer to the family all along. And I pussy-footed close enough to that porch to hunker in the dark and hear their talk. That's why I'm sure. They talked about Hammond's will."

"So, when Hammond goes . . . "

"She inherits. She gets it all. But what would that little college-educated gal know about runnin' a big cattle outfit? Not a damn thing."

"By then — or soon afterward — Anna will have a husband to relieve her of all responsibility." Dortweil chuckled complacently. "All the business details she could never understand."

"When the time comes, we can rig it to look like an accident," said Rushford.

"That's one idea," Dortweil agreed. "But accidents aren't easily arranged."

"There's other ways," Rushford assured him.

"Which all add up to murder," countered Dortweil. "And I'm sure you haven't forgotten my golden rule, Ed. I've never yet been a murder suspect and I don't intend starting now. When I put a man down, it has to be a no risk operation."

"We can do better than that," grinned Rushford. "With Burt and our other old buddies for witnesses, we can lay the whole thing at Frecker's door."

"A Circle 6 man identified as the killer," mused Dortweil. "Yes, I like that."

"Can be done," Rushford said confidently. "A lot of bad blood right now, Hammond hollerin' for Sun Basin water, Frecker holdin' out on him. I've got Diamond H riders fazin' Circle 6 waddies, raisin' hell with Frecker's nighthawks, givin' 'em a real bad time."

"Retaliation," smiled Dortweil. "Very satisfactory, Ed. The local law would buy it?"

"If they'd had bone-head sheriffs like Tarren in Kansas," said Rushford, "me and the boys'd still be there. We'd never have needed to cut and run for Nebraska."

"Short on imagination, this Tarren," guessed Dortweil.

"He's easily fooled," said Rushford. "We just don't have to worry about Phil Tarren."

"It's looking good," Dortweil decided. "Everything going according to plan and both Hammond and Frecker playing into our hands. So, for the present, we can afford to wait."

"But not for long," muttered Rushford. "Unless there's rain in three-four days, Hammond's gonna be desperate enough to do somethin' rash."

"Open warfare between Diamond H

and the Frecker crowd should provide the ideal opportunity," enthused Dortweil. "You're right, Ed. Diamond H is as good as ours."

"Meanwhile, we keep on makin' life miserable for Frecker's chicken-livered herders," said Rushford. "Burt and the boys gonna be ridin' again — tonight."

★ ★ ★

Already, the Circle 6 bunkhouse seemed almost like home to the new hands. Not that they were seeking a permanent roost. But, for the spring, Circle 6 would do. That bunkhouse put them in mind of other such retreats they had known in their earlier years.

At supper with the other hands that evening, with the ramrod presiding at the head of the table, they sampled Roscoe's beef stew, traded wistful grins and covertly studied the room's familiar appointments. Hung over every bunk, along with the owner's long gun, was the traditional horseshoe. The walls were tar-papered part way around, other sections being covered with old newspaper, illustrations out of Sears Roebuck catalogs and the like. Mingling with the aroma of Roscoe's stew were the lingering odors of tobacco, leather, tallow candles, coal-oil and sweat; in such surroundings they would never feel alien.

The meal was nearing its end when the ranch-boss paid an unscheduled visit. Dab came trudging across the threshhold in his shirtsleeves, helped himself to a spare chair, complained of the lack of a relieving breeze, cussed Roscoe for offering him a shot of his latest alcoholic masterpiece, then called for his employees' attention.

"Listen up now. Reverend Pickard's boy delivered an invite a couple hours ago, so we got to be polite and do some thinkin' on it."

"Invite he calls it, that sin-killer?" challenged Orv. "Tryin' to drum up trade for his Sunday meetin's, huh?"

"Nope, that ain't it at all," said Dab.

73

"How long since they held a social in Loomis? Hell, I can't remember the last one. And Sam Pickard's decided it's just what this county needs, a regular social with dancin' and bowls of punch and all you bucks slicked up in your best duds, the women rigged in their fanciest gowns. Folks socializin' and havin' fun, he says."

"I don't know if anybody feels like . . . " began Orv.

"That's why they're organizin' this shindig, and in the town hall, so there'll be plenty room for as many as comes," explained Dab. "The Reverend and his lady figure this is gonna be good for Loomis at a time like this, a chance for folks to shake off their miseries, forget the drought, enjoy 'emselves. And I'm agreein' with 'em. Dammit, the drought took the heart out of Loomis. Folks are forgettin' how to smile, to laugh, kick up their heels and let off a little steam."

"You gonna be there, Mister Frecker?" asked Shorty.

"*Gotta* be there," growled Dab. "My women're gigglin' and cluckin' in Desdemona's bedroom already, tryin' on their best gowns and plannin' how they're gonna purty up and dance 'emselves bone-weary. You think I could let 'em go without me?" He eyed the hands sternly. "Next Saturday night. So? Who's goin' and who's weaselin' out?"

Uncomfortable glances were exchanged by all but two of the bunkhouse gang.

"I don't dance so good," mumbled Elroy.

"Well, *I* sure as hell ain't gonna be there," sneered Roscoe. "Wouldn't be anybody there I'd take kindly to. I don't like nobody and . . ."

"You've been sayin' that for years," chided Dab.

"And, if I went, I'd have to socialize with folks," the cook sourly pointed out. "And that'd make me sick to my belly."

"My dancin' days are long past," sighed Orv. "At my age, a man just can't handle all that jiggin' and stompin'. Why, I could flop and die half-way through a square dance, flop right there on the floor with everybody lookin'. And that'd be mighty undignified."

"You knuckle-headed jackass," jeered Dab. "Old, you call yourself? I'm gonna be there for the dancin', aim to do my share of fancy steppin' with Addy. And you know damn well I could give you a year or two, maybe three."

"It mightn't be all that sociable," fretted Shorty. "Not if the Diamond H bunch shows up."

"It's a Saturday social I'm talkin' about," scowled Dab. "Not a saloon brawl." He stared hard at Shorty. "You'd get to dance with Lucy Lou — or ain't you interested?"

"Well — I dunno," shrugged Shorty.

"How can we have a good time with Hammond hard cases all around us?" grouched Fat Pat.

"Somethin' you bucks better think about," Dab grimly warned. "When a cattleman takes his women to a social, some of his hired hands always ride escort and join the festivities. Kyle Hammond'll be there for sure, him and his sister and a whole passel of Diamond H riders. If none of you got the gizzard for it, I'll still be there. I'll take Addy and my girls to town in our surrey and, after Saturday night, I'll be plumb ashamed of them that wouldn't side me." On an afterthought, he shifted his gaze to the tall men sipping coffee. "Near forgot you two. You leery of dancin'?"

"Wouldn't seem polite to turn down the invite," drawled Larry. "Mister Emerson, suh, you partial to the notion of showin' off for the ladies of Loomis, a little socializin', a little fancy struttin'?"

"Well now, Mister Valentine, suh," beamed Stretch. "Could I disappoint all them purty females, deprive 'em of the pleasure of my elegant steppin'?"

"Wouldn't be fair to the ladies," Larry gravely agreed. "But don't forget to take off your spurs. You did a Mexican hat dance around some poor hombre's brand-new sombrero a long time back and plumb tore it apart. That was in Gomez, New Arizona, as I recall."

"You have to tell everybody?" challenged Stretch.

"Forgot them spurs again in Bulmer, Colorado," grinned Larry. "Dancin' with the sheriff's wife, damned if you didn't snag a spur in her ball gown — tore it right off of the lady. And there she stood in her underduds, screamin' up a storm."

"We got run out of town that time," sighed Stretch. "I never been so ashamed."

These recollections triggered an outburst of mirth from Dab and the other men; even Roscoe abandoned his surliness to loose a wheezy chuckle. Rising to leave, Dab nodded amiably to the Texans and declared.

"I don't believe a word you said, but I'm damn glad we'll have your company at the social. Saturday night. Be duded up and ready to move about half after six. Addy likes a slow trip when she's wearin' her best gown. That way, we don't collect so much dust."

After their boss left them, the three cowboys began having second thoughts.

"I might go along after all," remarked Shorty. "I mean, if I ask her polite, Lucy Lou just got to dance with me, right?"

"And maybe them Hammond hard cases'll stay clear of us," Fat Pat said hopefully. "They'll see Larry and Stretch and — uh — they'll be rememberin' what happened at Farley Creek."

"Yeah, well, maybe I'll change my mind too," muttered Elroy. "Guess I'll feel a whole lot safer with Larry and Stretch along."

"Gettin' near time, Shorty," the ramrod announced.

"Oh, sure," nodded Shorty, rising. "Best get ready."

"If you're feelin' brave, slap a saddle

on Whitey," leered Fat Pat.

"That'll be the day," retorted Shorty. "Bravery ain't enough. Man'd have to be crazy."

Again the disquiet took hold of the Texans. After supper, lolling on their bunks and half-listening to the mumbled conversation of Fat Pat and Elroy, they thought of Diamond H and the intimidating influence brought to bear on the hands of Circle 6. They liked Shorty, Fat Pat and Elroy, but could not feel at ease with them. Doggedly cowardly men made them nervous. If the hands decided to attend Saturday night's big dance at the Loomis town hall, this would be no indication of new courage, defiance of Diamond H. They would go only because the new hands were going and only because the new hands had defeated double their number in Hammond hard cases at Farley Creek. Larry couldn't feel contempt for them. Just pity.

At 10 p.m., peeled down to their

Long Johns, Fat Pat and Elroy snored in their bunks. The Texans, still fully dressed, squatted side by side in the bunkhouse doorway, smoking their last cigarettes and staring out into the night, sharing a companionable silence. Roscoe had locked himself in his still beyond his cook-shack. Also still awake were the head of the Frecker family and his ramrod, talking quietly on the ranch-house porch.

Up along the basin's north slope, Shorty Rudge guided his climbing pony clear of a boulder and moved up to the level ground beyond the rim. He reined up, hooked a leg about his saddlehorn and fished out his makings. When he lit his quirley, he had to cup his hands about the match. The wind was blowing from the west, not a guster, but steady, a dry wind, no hint of moisture to it.

"Damn lousy drought," he mumbled.

His cigarette was half-smoked when he heard the thudding of hooves. Riders were advancing through the dry brush

81

100 yards west. He froze in his saddle, his scalp crawling. Seconds later, when the five riders emerged from the brush to race their mounts toward him, he groaned in dismay. A fearsome sight they were in the clear moonlight. Every rider was shrouded in a duster and masked by a floursack hood kept in place by his hat, and every rider brandished a six-gun. He tried to cry out, but his throat was suddenly as dry as the surrounding terrain and the dust kicked up by the raiders' horses — and now they had sighted him.

The night air filled with their blood-chilling war-whoops and the booming of their pistols and, at last, he rallied from his shock and took flight, wheeling his pony and starting down the slant. Bullets whined about him as he drew level with the boulder. In desperation, he pitched from his horse and crawled for the protection of the rock.

The Texans were on their feet while the first gunshot still echoed. Fat Pat jerked awake and blinked incredulously, startled by the speed of their movements. To their bunks they dashed to grab shell-belts and sheathed Winchesters, and then they were out of the bunkhouse and running for the barn.

From the ranch-house porch, Orv bellowed to the hands to saddle up and make ready to control the herd. By the time Fat Pat and Elroy were struggling into their pants, Larry and Stretch had readied the sorrel and pinto and were hustling them out of the barn, swinging astride. For the north slope they started, heeling their mounts to speed.

Reaching the base of the slope, they didn't slacken the pace. The well-rested and raring-to-go horses made the ascent fast, their riders scanning the area above, grimly resenting what they now saw. The five hooded horsemen were silhouetted atop the basin-rim, their six-shooters belching fire as they snapped shots at the hapless Shorty. He stayed huddled behind a rock barely big enough to shield him, .45 slugs bouncing off it, ricocheting, screaming like souls in torment.

"Scare raid," Stretch said bitterly.

"Real brave heroes," scowled Larry. "Five against one."

"Ain't spotted us yet," called Stretch, as they urged their mounts onward and upward. "Havin' their fun keepin' Shorty pinned back of that rock."

"We're close enough to faze 'em," Larry estimated.

"Not with our hoglegs," argued Stretch. "We ain't close enough for that."

"We ain't just packin' handguns, big feller," retorted Larry.

"Ain't that the truth!" chuckled Stretch.

From where he huddled and sweated in fear for his life, Shorty gaped at the tall riders hustling their animals up the slant. He saw them grip their reins in their teeth, unsheathe their Winchesters and ready them for action without easing their pace. And then they were coming on, charging past him with their rifles barking rapidly.

Suddenly, the raiders were suffering some of their own medicine, scattering wildly, frantic to get clear of the rim. Rifle-slugs were coming too close for comfort. A man loosed a wail of shock and pain and, through the eyeholes of his hood, gaped at the slash of red at his left upper arm.

"Dammit t' hell — I'm hit . . . !"

Another man experienced the belly-chilling sensation of a bullet whisking his hat away, a bullet that did all but tear his scalp. He felt the heat of it and caught the pungent odor of his singed hair and the burning of burlap as he dismounted to retrieve his headgear; that perforated Stetson had a distinctive snakeskin band well-known hereabouts.

"Fall back!" he snarled. "Make for the brush!"

Remounting hastily, he led his four cohorts in a wild dash away from Sun Basin. Shorty found his voice, yelling a plea to the tall men.

"Don't go after 'em! Yonder of the rim, you'll be clear targets!"

But, their blood up, the Texans urged their horses up to level ground to sight the retreating five and to pursue, reloading as they raced across the flats toward the brush. From its east end, just before following his companions into the brush, the wearer of the holed Stetson drew rein long enough for a backward glance.

"I'm gonna remember you bastards," he promised himself.

The pursuer with the broader shoulders rose in his stirrups with his Winchester barking. The man felt the tugging sensation at the brim of his Stetson.

"So you're the hat-shooter, huh? The hell with you!"

He triggered his last two shots at the hard-riding Texans and charged his mount into the brush, moving westward against the wind. Some minutes later, overtaking his cronies at the west end, he ordered a halt.

"They're still after us!" protested

the wounded man. "Hell, Burt, we should've brought *our* rifles! They got the edge on us!"

"*We* got the edge!" The man called Burt delved into his saddlebag to produce an out-dated issue of the Lommis newspaper. He began distributing sheets. "This brush'll burn fast — and right at 'em. Wind's blowin' their way. They could *fry* — and I hope they *do*! You jaspers get it burnin' north and south, then I'll light up this side! Hustle now!"

Again, the raiders scattered. Burt Marcus rid himself of his hood, waited for the brush to flare north and south, laughed harshly and fished out a match. He scratched it to life on his holster, touched it to a twist of newspaper, tossed it and urged his mount to movement. Tinder-dry, the tangle of brush began crackling. Flame spurted, upward at first, then eastward, spread fast by the wind.

While the five raced their horses clear of the blazing growth, still fleeing westward, the Texans, three-quarter way through the brush, jerked their mounts to a halt. They had sighted the danger signals.

"Sonsabitches," breathed Stretch.

"Fired the brush." Larry swore explosively. "Dead ahead and both sides of us." He twisted in his saddle. "Only one way we can head."

"Sure — back where we started from," muttered Stretch, as they wheeled their mounts. "Question is, can we get out in time?"

"We stay here and burn — or we give it our best shot," growled Larry. "Let's go!"

They sheathed their Winchesters and sank spur. The sorrel and pinto toted them through the brush at a hard gallop and their ordeal began. From either side, they were bedeviled by heat and choking smoke and flying fragments, blazing particles carried by the wind. Stung by sparks, the horses nickered in alarm, close to panic.

At ground level it was wildfire, the

surviving grass as dry as the brush. Once, darting a wary glance over his shoulder, Stretch felt his gorge rise. The fire was actually pursuing them and at frightening speed, a whole wall of flame less than 6 yards to their rear.

The sorrel stumbled and almost went down, struggled up again and charged on. Larry cursed luridly and, one-handed, unknotted and got rid of his bandana; it was smoldering. Stretch felt the fiery impact of 3 feet of flaring brush descending on his shoulders, thrust it away and felt his left sleeve burning. Before the flames could reach his undershirt and flesh, he got his right hand to his left shoulder, grasped at the material and tore the whole sleeve away.

And then, after what seemed an eternity, they were outrunning the inferno threatening them from north, south and rear; the as yet surviving east edge was straight ahead and, beyond it, the basin-rim.

Moving across the flats, they spared

no backward glance. Every inch of that vast clump was afire; they didn't need to look back. They knew they had gotten out of there with less than a minute to spare. Now they could slow their panting animals to a walk.

The danger past — but not forgotten — Larry cursed again and began brooding. Stretch, after his first mighty sigh of relief, waxed philosophical.

"They near parboiled us, but we sure as hell fazed 'em."

"I don't even know if we drew blood," grouched Larry.

"Me neither," shrugged Stretch. "But, the way they scattered, I figure we scared 'em bad." He winced and scratched at his chest. "I itch. Got holes burned in my duds and my skins black-streaked. Cool water in the lake sure gonna feel good."

"I'm for that," said Larry. "But later. Best we tend the horses first. They've earned a rub-down and their hides'll need greasin' where the brush burned 'em."

Reaching the rim, they began their descent. Shorty reappeared, mounted now and more than a little in awe of them.

"Hot damn," he breathed. "I never seen nothin' like that before — the way you come chargin' up here . . . "

"Herd's peaceable, huh?" asked Larry, surveying the basin floor.

"Too well-fed to turn ornery," said Shorty. "I never figured they'd stampede anyway."

"That's somethin' you don't take bets on," countered Larry.

"They score on you, them night-raiders?" demanded Stretch.

"Well, no," frowned Shorty, falling in beside them. "Lucky for me I made it to that rock. Listen — uh — I sure appreciate what you fellers did for me."

"Forget it," grunted Larry.

"What is that?" challenged Shorty, looking them over. "Your duds are all black and burned . . . "

"After we chased 'em into the brush,

91

they set it afire," said Stretch "We near got our butts burnt off."

"Them Diamond H waddies got to be the meanest bunch of . . . " began Shorty.

"You know for sure they were Diamond H?" countered Larry. "You could see behind them hoods?"

"Who else could they be?" frowned Shorty.

"They were likely Diamond H," said Larry. "But how do we prove it if we couldn't see their faces?"

Dab, Orv and the other hands awaited them by the bunkhouse. They reined up and, not waiting for the rancher's questions, offered a terse account of their misadventure.

"You got somethin' for these burns?" Stretch asked the cook, gesturing to the spent sorrel and pinto. "After we've rubbed 'em down we'll need to soothe 'em some, else they'll smart like all get-out."

"Yeah, I'll fetch somethin'," nodded Roscoe.

"Seems like they ain't lettin' up on us, Dab," muttered Orv.

"I never swore no complaint against Hammond, never yet ran to the county law for help," Dab said grimly. "Can't accuse Diamond H anyway, not if them raiders was tricked out in hoods. But, this time, I'm callin' the law in. Damn it, my two best men near got killed tonight, near got burned alive."

"Don't fret on our account," said Larry.

"It ought to be done just the same," insisted Dab. "I'm goin' inside and write a note to Sheriff Tarren. Least he can do is come out and investigate — or whatever it is a lawman's supposed to do. Why shouldn't Phil Tarren earn what he's paid from our taxes?"

"Sounds reasonable," shrugged Orv.

"Roscoe'll be takin' the wagon in early for supplies," said Dab. "I'll have him deliver my note to Tarren." As the Texans began leading their mounts away, he made them an offer. "Fat Pat and Elroy could tend your

93

animals. You boys're lookin' plenty toilworn."

"Thanks, but we'll tend our own critters," said Stretch.

With the tall men out of earshot, Dab issued firm orders.

"Orv, let Larry and Stretch sleep late. Roscoe, I don't want to hear any bellyachin' from you if they ain't up for breakfast. And, when they do rise out of their bunks, you make sure you're ready to feed 'em, savvy?"

"The heroes of Circle 6," jibed Roscoe.

"None of your back-talk," scowled Dab. "With a half-dozen of their kind, I could beat the hell out of the whole Hammond outfit — if I had to." He turned on his heel. "I'm goin' right in and write that damn note."

Stripped to nought but their boots, towels knotted about their middles, the Texans swabbed and rubbed down their horses, watched by the profoundly impressed Shorty Rudge and his cohorts.

"You got spare duds?" frowned

94

Elroy. "What you just took off ain't gonna be no more use to you."

"We tote an extra shirt and Levis apiece," Stretch said offhandedly.

"Best get us some new stuff for the Saturday dance," decided Larry. "I'll slip Roscoe enough dinero 'fore he heads for town in the mornin'." He called to the cook. "Roscoe? We're ready to grease these burns."

It was 11.25 p.m. by the time the sorrel and pinto, calmer now and with the smarting of their burns easing, were returned to their stalls. Toting soap, the Texans then trudged through the moonlight to the lake. They were dog-tired, experiencing a delayed reaction to their ordeal, but loath to retire before ridding themselves of dust and soot.

Gratefully, they tugged off their boots, rid themselves of towels and waded into the water. At once their tension subsided. They dunked their tired frames and set about soaping themselves, hunkering in the shallows.

"Circle 6 gonna be a safe roost for us," mumbled Stretch. "That's what we figured. We stay out of the Loomis saloons, just hang around this spread, tend our chores and earn our pay, we'll be just a couple ranch-hands with no worries."

"That's what we figured," nodded Larry.

"We oughtn't of signed on with Dab," fretted Stretch. "We hexed Circle 6. Anyplace we go, there's just bound to be gun-trouble."

"Guess again," growled Larry. "This time, we don't have to blame ourselves. Diamond H was spookin' Circle 6 long before we came to Loomis County."

"Oh, sure," frowned Stretch. "I plumb forgot."

"You had your fill of ranch-livin' already, wantin' to quit?" asked Larry.

Stretch grinned through a mask of lather while soaping his unruly thatch.

"You know me, runt. I don't never quit. Not till *you* quit."

"I should hope," said Larry.

"And you ain't about to quit," guessed Stretch.

"Two things I plan on doin'," confided Larry. "Help out at round-up and join the drive to Omaha. That's one thing. And the other thing is, when I'm good and ready, I want to pow wow with Mister High-And-Mighty Hammond. Eyeball to eyeball."

"On account of . . . ?" prodded Stretch.

"I aim to be mighty sure about him — mighty sure he knows what kind of trigger-happy scum ride for him."

"Why wouldn't he know? He's the boss."

"They tried to burn us alive. And that makes me plenty curious."

"Didn't make me all that curious. Just scared hell out of me." Stretch submerged for a long moment, rose up spluttering and conceded, "On the other hand, you was born curious."

"When I'm good and ready," Larry

repeated. "We'll talk. Hammond and me."

Stretch wallowed contentedly, conscious the evening night breeze was dry and warm but the Sun Basin water cool and refreshing. It was a good feeling. He was savoring it, until he rose to his full height, glanced toward the ranch-house and spotted the wraith-like figures.

His startled gasp demanded Larry's attention.

"What the hell . . . ?"

"Ghosts!"

"Hogwash. There's no such thing as . . ."

"Look there — headed right for us!"

Larry, in water up to his navel, put wary eyes on the approaching figures, both of them clear in the moonlight, the night wind catching their long hair and fluttering the light robes they wore over their sleeping garments. He grimaced irritably.

"They ain't ghosts," he growled. "They're Dab's young'uns."

"Hey, this is mortifyin'," fretted Stretch.

"Deb's college-educated, husband-huntin' daughters," scowled Larry, as they retreated from the lake's edge.

4

Love And Deputy Allsop

TO Larry's chagrin and Stretch's dismay, the sisters Frecker advanced to the soft grass by the lake's edge and seated themselves gracefully.

"We were so *concerned* for you," Desdemona began.

"So *terribly* concerned," smiled Lucy Lou.

"The noise awakened us," explained Desdemona. "We heard Papa telling Mama about your terrible ordeal and we just had to be sure you weren't seriously injured."

"That's right friendly of you young ladies," said Larry, who chose to tight-rein his temper, at least for the moment. "Now — uh — excuse me for mentionin' it, but my partner and me are hunkerin' here buck-naked. Like you can see, we weren't expectin' company."

"This is humiliatin'," complained Stretch. "I ain't never felt so embarrassed."

"But you don't have to be embarrassed," smiled Desdemona.

"Certainly not on *our* account," Lucy Lou assured them.

"Holy Hannah! I shouldn't be embarrassed?" Stretch eyed them aghast. "Ladies, this ain't proper! You're female and we ain't."

"They likely know that already," suggested Larry.

"We aren't foolish, immature girls," Desdemona pointed out. "We are enlightened."

"And progressive — and scornful of stodgy convention," giggled Lucy Lou.

"That's what college-learnin' did for you?" challenged Larry. "What's enlightened mean?"

"Greater freedom of thought — the urge to take one's place in society as a woman of imagination and independent mind," said Desdemona. "Heavens, Mister Valentine, we have studied art and biology. We're quite blase about the male in his naked state."

"And terribly attracted to you," said Lucy Lou. "I think Stretch is so cute — in his homespun way. And Desdemona . . ."

"I feel drawn to you, Larry," declared Desdemona. "Yes, I feel a rapport — also some tantalizing impulses. You see? We speak freely, unashamedly, of our emotions. That, Larry, is typical of the enlightened woman."

"The woman of today and the future," enthused Lucy Lou. "So much more broad-minded, more progressive, than the down-trodden women of the frontier — poor souls."

"You savvy *any* of that gab?" Stretch worriedly enquired of his partner.

"I'm tryin' hard," muttered Larry. "But it ain't easy."

"We have many qualities that must appeal to you," Desdemona assured him. "We are skilled in the domestic arts. We are willing and eager for matrimony — oh, so eager, so starved for affection."

"We're really *ready*," chuckled Lucy Lou.

"They sure are ready, runt," fretted Stretch.

"No argument," grinned Larry. "Ladies, let me ask you somethin'. You ever talk this way to the gents that come callin' on you?"

"Certainly not," frowned Desdemona. "It would only confuse them."

"I'd reckon it'd get 'em plenty interested," drawled Larry. "Anyway, you're makin' your pitch at the wrong hombres."

"You are bachelors and so strong, so appealing," Lucy Lou said blissfully. "And you're *here*!"

"We ain't as bachelor as you think," countered Larry, jerking a thumb to indicate the self-conscious Stretch. "My partner's got a couple squaws in Wyomin' and another in Nevada and I dunno how many papooses.

Got a white wife in Salina, New Mexico too. And me, I'd be no use to you. I'm apt to sleepwalk any time of night. And, when I sleepwalk, I head straight for the nearest cat-house."

"*Really*!" gasped Lucy Lou.

"I don't believe a word of that," protested Desdemona.

"Much obliged," mumbled Stretch. "Pay no mind to his joshin'."

"Be serious, Larry," urged Desdemona.

"Have it your way," shrugged Larry. "And listen close now, because this is plenty serious. We're *stayin'* bachelor, the beanpole and me."

"We admire women, but . . ." began Stretch.

"But we never met a woman deserves the kind of misery we'd give her," declared Larry. "Women need a home-place. Women need to be good and settled, strong roof over their heads, strong walls and a strong man to protect 'em. What they *don't* need is the likes of us, a couple fiddlefoots with the wander-itch. When I tell you we have to keep movin', ladies, I ain't whistlin' Dixie."

"It's the pure truth," Stretch assured them.

"Can't stop driftin', can't ever quit," said Larry. "So don't waste your time on us."

Crestfallen, the younger sister remarked, "They sound very definite about it, Desdemona."

"So all I got for you gals is advice," offered Larry. "But I don't reckon you'd be interested. After all, you're a whole lot smarter'n a tearaway like me. What do *I* know? I ain't college-educated."

"Don't be sarcastic," chided Desdemona. "It's unbecoming."

"What kind of advice?" asked Lucy Lou.

"What kind of advice?" asked Desdemona.

"Stay patient," urged Larry. "You got a lot of years ahead of you and there'll be many a deservin' man courtin' you. Just don't spook 'em, savvy?"

"Spook them?" frowned Desdemona.

"It's supposed to be the man does the huntin'," said Larry. "Any man you talk to — the way you been talkin' to us — he'll spook and run, nothin' surer."

"I guess they're saying we're too pushy," murmured Lucy Lou.

"Larry sounds just like Papa," complained Desdemona, pouting.

"Listen now," Larry said casually. "How about these bucks that's tryin' to court you right now? How come you don't encourage 'em?"

"Shorty Rudge — for *me*?" sniffed Lucy Lou. "The very idea."

"He's the kind that'd never run out on you," he assured her. "Real steady, young Shorty. Got sand too."

"Sand indeed," jibed Lucy Lou. "He's scared of those Diamond H hooligans."

"Too bad you didn't see him up there by the basin-rim when them hooded gunhawks came a'raidin'," said Larry.

"When the chips're down, Shorty's a fightin' fool," lied Stretch.

"I've heard it said there's a man for every woman," Larry remarked to Desdemona.

"Well, Toddy Allsop is not the man for *this* woman," she retorted. "He's homely and clumsy. I should encourage *him*? I should say not." She heaved a sigh. "The *other* deputy . . . "

"She means Grant Symes, the handsome one," offered Lucy Lou.

"My pulse quickens at the sight of him," smiled Desdemona.

"But he don't know you're alive," guessed Larry.

"That's a cruel thing to say!" she bridled.

"Ever think of settlin' for the man that wants you most?" he challenged. "If this Allsop hombre got a real hankerin' for you, ain't he then your best chance?"

"He's ugly," argued Desdemona.

107

"So am I," declared Larry. Again, he jerked a thumb. "I've been jawin' to you frisky females, squattin' in this water and wonderin' how long you're gonna hang around — and now I'm through waitin'. Ugly is what's gonna happen, if I have to climb out of here and paddle your tail."

"He'll do it!" Stretch warned the sisters. "Don't sass him no more. I've *seen* him do it — time and time again!"

"Now scat," ordered Larry. "Vamoose!"

"Don't you just love it when Larry becomes masterful?" enthused Lucy Lou.

"I suppose we should leave them," shrugged Desdemona, rising from the grass, tossing her head. "They really are old-fashioned you know — drearily conservative, unimaginative, unenlightened . . ."

"And out of patience!" warned Larry.

"We're going," Lucy Lou assured them. "We're going!"

She rose and, with her sister, began hurrying back to the ranch-house. It was time for the taller Texan to give voice to his humiliation again, and he did so.

"That spooked me clear to my bones, runt. That was spookier'n ridin' through that fire. Them just a'settin' there — gab, gab, gab, gab — and us bare-assed. Hell! It ain't decent!"

Emerging from the lake, they towelled themselves dry, knotted the towels about their waists and re-donned their boots. Larry was grinning again, his exasperation forgotten.

"Just goes to prove somethin'," he mused, as they steered a course for the bunkhouse. "College-educated they are, but too damn foolish, too dumb to look any further than a good-lookin' face and a few muscles."

"Howzat again?" frowned Stretch.

"Looks!" shrugged Larry. "A hombre as handsome as this deputy — what'd she call him . . . ?"

"Grimes," said Stretch. "Sam Grimes."

"Grant Symes," corrected Larry.

"Whatever," shrugged Stretch.

"Is Symes gonna stay handsome all his life?" challenged Larry. "Is Desdemona gonna stay so all-fired purty? *Nobody* does. Looks don't last. Men get older and so do women. Husband's lose their hair, maybe their teeth. Wives get fat or maybe scrawny. He ain't handsome no more and she ain't purty. But it don't matter a damn, not if they got hitched for the right reasons."

"Pardon me for remindin' you," said Stretch. "You ain't never gonna be no woman's husband, so how come you savvy all about marriage?"

"It don't take a college education," Larry assured him. "All it takes is horse-sense, plain savvy. Dab and Addy now, they're happy enough on account of they get along. Gettin' along is what counts, know what I mean? When they got into double harness, chances are Dab was a right slick-lookin' young feller and Addy as purty as paint, but that ain't why they got wed. Hell, no. They figured they'd get used to each other. They were pretty sure they'd get along. It's what kind of two-legged critter you are. It ain't how you look. Looks don't matter. Looks ain't worth a hill o' beans."

"I guess you're right," said Stretch.

"You know I'm right and I know I'm right," complained Larry. "So how come them fool females are so wrong? And them college-educated!"

"Sure beats all," shrugged Stretch.

"Ain't that the truth," said Larry.

* * *

At breakfast next morning, rigged in their other shirts and Levis, the survivors of last night's violence tucked money into the same pocket of Roscoe's vest containing Dab's note for the sheriff.

"Couple respectable shirts, couple pairs of pants, Roscoe," said Larry.

"What size . . ." began the cook.

"You need to ask?" challenged Stretch. "Biggest in the store."

It promised to be another day of dry, ennervating heat, an extension of the freak weather pattern that had frayed the nerves of townmen concerned about the local economy and soured the dispositions of Diamond H riders striving to control a herd threatened by a dwindling water supply.

There were two bunkhouses at Diamond H, both located a fair distance from the imposing Hammond home. The larger building housed the bulk of the crew. The smaller building had 8 bunks and was the exclusive retreat of the foreman and the five cohorts who had followed him out of Kansas some 18 months before. Ed Rushford lounged in the doorway of that bunkhouse and traded talk with these men at about the same time Roscoe Cully drove the ranch wagon out of Sun Basin and began his journey to the country seat.

For the first time, a scare raid on

Circle 6 had backfired. The burly, shaggy-browed Burt Marcus had returned from that raid with an embarrassing reminder of the debacle and one man wounded. No doctor had been summoned. The bullet-gashed arm was bandaged and the bandage concealed by the sleeve of a fresh shirt, the blood-stained garment burned.

"First time they've hit back," remarked Rushford. "But I'm not worryin', Burt. All it proves is they're gettin' jumpier — and that's how I want 'em."

"Frecker hired a couple new hands," opined Marcus. He was squatting on his bunk, glowering into a mirror. "It wasn't Hagenthorpe and the fat boy came at us with rifles."

"No matter," grinned the man with the arm-wound. "We sure paid 'em off."

"Maybe they burned and maybe they didn't," scowled Marcus. "They could've got lucky and made it to the east end of the brush and back to the basin."

113

"Couple sharpshooters, good with rifles," mused Rushford. "Well now, that could work for us. When the time's right, I might decide the big boss should be hit from long range — with a rifle slug. Don't worry, Burt. Everything's goin' our way."

He grinned wryly as he added, "And don't be frettin' about your looks."

"Easy for you to talk!" snapped Marcus. "How'd you like to look like this?"

He turned face-on to the ramrod, who wisely resisted the impulse to laugh. Burt Marcus was lucky to be alive, but didn't appreciate his narrow escape. This surely was the closest of close shaves. There were now two parts in his hair. The new one was a full inch wide and extended from the hairline on the right side clear to the top of the cranium. The hair about that furrow was singed. The effect was dramatic and, to Rushford's eye, also comical. But not to Marcus, still seething, hungering for vengeance.

"It'll grow back," shrugged Rushford. "Try brushin' it the other way."

"Hammond know about last night?" another man asked.

"All he knows is we fazed 'em again," said Rushford. "He ain't interested in details right now." He winked slyly. "Busy with other doin's — such as playin' host to this special guest."

"We'd of gotten rich faster in Kansas," Marcus said irritably. "All this waitin' . . . "

"You know what we're waitin' for and you know it's worth the waitin'," growled Rushford. "In Kansas, we risked our hides raidin' stagecoaches and the pickin's weren't all that fat, Burt. This deal is easier, safer for us."

"It's a big outfit, sure," growled Marcus. "But, without water, it'll be wiped out. Diamond H stock won't be worth ten cents a head. Some of 'em are near ready to drop."

"Drought can't last forever," said Rushford. "And, if it don't damn

115

soon rain around here, Hammond'll go haywire, give us the word to run the whole herd into Sun Basin."

"That's what I crave." Marcus's voice shook as he made his declaration. "Us hittin' Circle 6 — with everything — and me gettin' a bead on the bastard that did *this* to me!"

He was glaring into the mirror again when Rushford walked away from the bunkhouse.

★ ★ ★

Having left Circle 6 at an early hour, Roscoe Cully drove into Loomis around 9 o'clock that morning. He stalled the wagon in front of Berkle's Mercantile, presented his list to the storekeeper and announced.

"While you're fillin' our order, I'll be visitin' the sheriff. Got business with him."

"Gonna file a complaint against the local saloon owners, Roscoe?" grinned Berkle. "Because their booze isn't as high-class as yours?"

"Laugh all you want, Lester Berkle," scowled Roscoe. "My time is comin'. You mind what I'm tellin' you. I'll damn soon cook up a rye whiskey that'll make every other brand taste like swill — which is all it is anyway."

He stamped out of the emporium and along to the sheriff's office and, without a word of greeting to the three lawmen present, tossed his boss's note onto Tarren's desk and stamped out again.

Obese and lazy, tending to be offhand nowadays, moon-faced Phil Tarren grinned derisively and remarked, "Moon-shine Cully's been and gone."

"And left you a little something," observed Grant Symes. Lean of build, neatly garbed and even-featured, he puffed on a cigar and propped a shoulder against the jamb of the cellblock entrance. The Loomis County Jail was a sizeable structure, double-storied, cellblocks on both floors. "If that's an insulting note written by

Cully himself, you could maybe call it an offense and let him cool his butt in a cell."

"You're too hard on Roscoe," complained the other deputy. "I don't know why everybody treats him that way. Personally, I get along fine with him."

Toddy Allsop was perched on the third step of the stairs leading to the second floor cellblock, a scruffy fellow when compared to this well-groomed colleague, tousle-haired, of unimpressive physique, a good enough deputy in his plodding way. His dearest friends, even his own mother, would never have called him handsome; the button nose, receding chin and buck-teeth were an unfortunate facial arrangement.

Tarren relaxed in his swivel-chair as he unfolded and read Dab Frecker's note. Not so relaxed, he grimaced resentfully and announced, "This is real trouble. I can't ignore this kind of demand from a cattleman."

"Frecker wrote the note?" asked Symes.

"Yeah, this is from Frecker," frowned Tarren. "We've been hearin' rumors of night-riders raisin' hell around Sun Basin, right? Frecker filed no complaint so I didn't have to take any action. But now he's complainin' — *plenty*."

"Anybody hurt at Circle 6?" Toddy was suddenly anxious.

"No thanks to the bunch that hit 'em last night," muttered Tarren. "Five hooded riders, it says here. Couple of Frecker's hands fought 'em off with rifles, chased 'em into the brush west of the basin and near got barbecued. Seems the raidin' party fired the brush and these two hotshots had 'emselves a real close call. Well now, that's serious." He looked at Symes. "So I got to send a deputy out to Circle 6 to — uh — conduct an investigation. Not much chance you'll find any clues, but we have to make the gesture."

"Send Toddy," Symes said quickly. "How come you're so nervous?"

challenged the sheriff.

"You know why, Phil," said Symes, wincing. "The way Desdemona Frecker keeps pushing herself at me . . . "

"You be damn careful how you talk about Desdemona, Grant Symes!" warned Toddy, as he got to his feet.

"Send Toddy," Symes repeated, and now he made it a frantic plea. "Whatever needs doing, he can do it. Why should it be me? If I go out there, she'll come at me like a she-wolf and I'll get the whole treatment again, the heavy breathing and the sweet talk and the glad eye . . . "

"Any red-blooded bachelor would give an arm to be admired by a girl like Desdemona. She's got class and dignity and — she's so all-fired purty."

"Keep your shirt on, Toddy," muttered Symes. "I got nothing to say against the lady's character. It's just that she's not for me. You know I got my eye on somebody else."

"You makin' any progress with Sheba

Gilliam?" grinned his boss.

"She's still playing hard to get," shrugged Symes. "But that's okay. Give me a choice and I'd rather chase Sheba than have to cut and run every time Desdemona catches sight of me." He appealed to Toddy. "You'd like to ride out there, wouldn't you, pal? Chance to make a big impression on her, let her see you on the job, conducting official business? Do yourself a favor, Toddy. Shine your badge, put on your best clothes and go bedazzle the lady." He turned to Tarren. "What do you say, Phil?"

"I ain't objectin' to takin' the assignment," mumbled Toddy.

"Glad to hear that — on account of you got it," Tarren said dryly. "But, hell, Toddy, you don't need your Sunday finery. You can just saddle up and ride right on out."

"No!" Toddy was adamant. "She's quality. I couldn't let her see me lookin' like a bum. I got to spruce up."

"Toddy, boy, no Loomis lawman ever looked like a bum," asserted Tarren who, on any of his off days, could be mistaken for a deadbeat. "But, if you got your heart set on it, do your damnedest and best foot forward. Just don't forget what you're there for, okay?"

"Grant, can I borrow your key?" begged Toddy.

"My key?" blinked Symes.

"To your room at Kerrigan's," Toddy said pleadingly; the deputies occupied adjoining quarters in a local room-and-board. "How else am I gonna get in there?"

"Get in there for what?" demanded Symes, fishing out the key.

"I need to borrow one of your genuine celluloid collars," said Toddy.

★ ★ ★

As he surrendered his key, Symes asked "You own a necktie? No, I didn't think so. All right, you'll find a blue polka dot in my top dresser drawer along with the collars."

"Thanks a lot, friend," grinned Toddy.

"All I ask," said Symes, as his colleague started out, "is don't mention my name to Desdemona."

Some 30 minutes after Roscoe Cully had loaded supplies and driven out of town, lovelorn Toddy Allsop mounted his horse and pointed it in the general direction of Sun Basin. The prospect of catching even a fleeting glimpse of the object of his affections was causing his pulse to race. With extreme care he had slicked down his unruly hair. He had flicked a little bay rum about his ears and jowls and donned his Sunday suit which, these past 6 months, had become a little tight on him. His floppy-brimmed felt hat had been discarded in favor of a tan derby which clashed with the rusty black of his suit, but he was relying on his borrowed neckwear to create an impression of sartorial elegance.

Roscoe returned to Circle 6 to find Dab and the hands assembled by the plank corral in which trigger-tempered Whitey, the as yet unbroken, cantankerous calico, was confined.

"What's goin' on?" he demanded, as he climbed down.

"Dab's decided it's past time this critter got to be a regular work-horse," drawled the ramrod.

"Time he earned his feed," growled Dab. "If there's one thing I can't abide, it's an ungrateful animal, and *this* animal's selfish through and through. Gets fed and watered regular, takes all he can get, but never gives nothin'."

"I'll tell you what he'll give, Boss," offered Fat Pat. "Bloody hell to any poor feller tries to ride him."

"He's got to be broke," insisted Dab. "And I want it done this very mornin'."

"I already tried and got throwed," Shorty reminded him.

"I sure don't want to sound like no coward," muttered Elroy, "but I just ain't got the nerve to straddle him."

"Never was a horse that couldn't be broke," said Larry.

"Prove it," challenged Elroy.

"Guess it has to be one of us, runt,' shrugged the taller Texan. "We flip for it?"

"Might's well," nodded Larry.

"All right now, let's do this fair and square," said Orv, producing a coin. "You fellers call, and then *I'll* flip 'er."

"Heads," said Larry.

"Tails," said Stretch.

Orv tossed and caught the coin, unclenched his hand and exhibited the dime.

"Tails. So it's up to you, Stretch."

"You can do it. This ain't the first wild one you licked." Larry imparted advice and encouragement as, hefting saddle and harness, he climbed into the corral with his partner, Fat Pat nervously following. "Now, you got nothin' to worry about, just so long as you . . ."

"Aw, c'mon now," chided Stretch. "Sure I can do it. You don't have to be leery of him. If I ain't spooked, why should *you* spook?"

"I don't trust him," muttered Larry, as they advanced warily. "Never trust a critter as mean-eyed as this one."

With half-hearted assistance from Fat Pat, the Texans began the struggle to prepare the outlaw for riding. In the process, Whitey almost got his teeth to Larry's shoulder, winning a reaction that startled the onlookers.

"You ever try that again . . . !" Larry dared the quivering forelegs by confronting the calico and backhanding his nose. He then glared into the animal's face. "Damn you, Whitey, I'll have me a mustang steak, so help me!"

Whitey flinched and, taking quick advantage, Fat Pat fitted the bridle and Stretch secured the cinch. After trading frowns with his foreman, Dab retreated toward the ranchhouse; he figured the porch was a more suitable vantagepoint from whence to view the coming battle.

And a whole lot safer. Orv, Shorty and Elroy backstepped a respectful distance from the corral and, sweating, the chubby cowpoke clambered out and hurried across to join them.

"That Larry," he said fervently. "Hey, he's plenty rough."

"I never saw a man do that before," mumbled Shorty. "Slap a mean horse right on the snoot."

"Ain't them Texans afeared of *anything*?" wondered Elroy.

"Might be they're just plain foolhardy," opined Orv.

The increasing tension was contagious. Addy Frecker and her daughters now joined Dab on the porch.

"How exciting!" cried Desdemona.

"Excitin' — yep," nodded Dab. "And dangerous. Plenty dangerous."

While Stretch made ready to swing astride, Larry controlled the calico as best as he could, temporarily blindfolding him by pressing his Stetson to his eyes, clutching the bridle with his free hand.

"Say when!" he called.

"Uh huh — okay . . . " Stretch planted his lean rump in the saddle, nudged his boots securely into the stirrups and took a firm grip of the rein. "Lemme have him — now!"

Larry let go, whisked his hat away and made a beeline for the nearest planks. He was vaulting out of the corral when, neighing shrilly, the white outlaw reared, forehooves pawing air. For a moment there it seemed certain he would fall backward out of sheer spite, hoping to crush his rider. Then the forehooves came pounding down and the back arched. He jack-knifed, he bucked, he hurled himself to left and right and Stretch was jolted and jerked but not thrown. His rebel yell infuriated the outlaw, starting him charging about the corral, raising dust-clouds. At intervals, he came to an abrupt, bone-jarring halt, and still Stretch stayed mounted.

"Look at that!" gasped Shorty.

"I never seen a mean critter with so

128

many mean tricks," declared Orv. "If he throws Stretch, it's for sure he'll stomp him."

"You think so?" Larry grinned mirthlessly. "Listen, if that crazy cayuse tried to stomp my partner, he will rise up and kick his butt — and you better believe it."

"How many wild ones has Stretch broken?" asked Fat Pat.

"Who keeps count?" shrugged Larry. "It's like gettin' shot at, amigo. After the first half-dozen bullets near score on you — you get used to it."

It was as violent a display as had ever been seen at Circle 6. Every treacherous trick in the book, plus many of his own invention, frustrated Whitey in his attempts to rid himself of a tough Texan determined to subdue him. He tried whirling like a dervish. He bucked and heaved without running out of steam and, in desperation, decided to transfer the battle to a larger arena. For the calico to attempt a flying leap from the corral would have been futile, and still he managed an exit.

"I don't — *believe* this . . . !" yelled Dab.

Whitey had carried Stretch to a section of the plank railing and was now lashing out with his hind hooves, wreaking havoc. Planks were shattered, fragments and splinters scattering in all directions, until those powerful hooves had cleared a jagged opening wide enough to permit passage.

"It's maybe a mite late for sayin' it," Larry dryly remarked to the ramrod. "Plank corral is no place for a mean horse. Better a strong *pole* corral."

"Now you tell us!" gasped Elroy.

"By golly — there they go!" cried Shorty.

Whitey had barged through the opening with Stretch still clinging and, probably supposing a fast gallop would unseat the taller Texan, was whirling and charging toward the south slope, charging at an oncoming rider, the hapless Deputy Allsop.

5

Plans For A Social Function

UP till now, the action had been fast and furious. From here on, it was fast, furious and confused. Understandably dismayed at the prospect of a head-on collision, the deputy's horse reared, almost throwing him. So did the calico. Stretch hauled back on the reins and, as the outlaw's forehooves left the ground, jerked relentlessly, forcing him to whirl on his hind legs.

Toddy Allsop's animal, craving the comforting company of other humans, now charged into the yard with the calico in hot pursuit and Toddy vainly attempting to restrain him. Orv and the hands, all but Larry, began beating a retreat toward the bunkhouse. To startle both animals into vacating the yard, Larry bellowed at them, drew his Colt and discharged it to the sky. The report momentarily surprised Whitey and, his whoops merging with Larry's bull-like roar, Stretch wheeled him again and hustled him around the corral.

Dab and spouse suddenly decided the ranch-house porch was no longer a safe vantagepoint. Still in panic, out of control, Toddy's animal barged to the steps and began climbing.

"Everybody inside!" cried Dab, grasping Addy by her tight-corsetted midriff and hustling her to the doorway.

"Don't worry about a thing, Mister Frecker!" gasped Toddy, as his mount carried him up to the porch. "I can handle this critter!"

"The hell you can!" retorted Dab.

He showed Addy inside, scampered in after her and, to the alarm of his daughters, forgot about them and slammed the door. The sisters cringed at the north end of the porch and loosed unladylike shrieks; Toddy's animal was clumping in their direction and, under these confused circumstances, looking twice as big as a horse ought to be. It was Toddy's big moment and he made the most of it, easing his boots from stirrups, swinging down, then moving in front of his trembling animal.

"You ladies just stay where you are," he cautioned with his back to the girls. "If this crazy critter tries to do you a harm, he's gonna have to kill me first!" He fixed a grim eye on his already subdued mount, one of the most malleable saddle animals in Loomis Country. "Back up, Lucifer, you murderin' varmint!" He retrieved his dangling rein. "C'mon now! Better forget about savagin' these beautiful ladies — specially Miss Desdemona. I'm takin' you off of this porch now. You try one wrong move — I'll start on you with my fists, I swear!"

"Sister, don't you just love it when Toddy becomes masterful?" panted Lucy Lou.

"Don't ask foolish questions," chided

Desdemona, "while I'm being terrified out of my wits!"

"Easy, Miss Desdemona," soothed Toddy. "The way I feel about you, I just got to do this. It'll be risky but — for your sake . . ."

He made a fine show of growling threats at his animal as he forced it to back along the porch to the area between the front door and the steps. There, in order to guide the horse down the steps, he was obliged to turn him. He did that just as Dab remembered he had left the girls out there. The door opened, Dab emerged and was buffeted by the rump of the wheeling horse and sent staggering back to collide with Addy.

"Get that damn critter out of here!" he raged.

"Don't speak so harshly to Deputy Allsop, Papa," cried Lucy Lou. "Not when he's being so terribly brave."

"I wouldn't have believed it!" gasped Desdemona.

Still growling impressive threats to

his bewildered horse, Toddy guided him down the steps and along to the hitchrail. While tethering the animal, he nodded to the sisters.

"No danger now, ladies. He knows better than to try any more devilry."

Unconcerned with the deputy's show of heroism, Larry and the hands were concentrating all their attention on the near-exhausted calico and the veteran too tough to be thrown. Stretch had maneuvered the outlaw back to the smashed section of the corral. Psychology was a word he could not spell nor understand, but psychology was what he was using right now. He cussed, cuffed with his Stetson and, with knees and heels, forced the snorting Whitey to re-enter the corral the way he had left it. And, once that was done, Whitey was a different animal; he got the point.

While the onlookers applauded, the horse and rider became immobile in the centre of the corral, Stretch still muttering reprimands, Whitey lathered and panting with his head down.

"All right, so I was rough on you," Stretch conceded. "But it's easier when you quit actin' ornery. Show you what I mean, Whitey ol' buddy. We'll trot some now, gentle as you please, real polite."

Before dismounting, he trotted the calico twice around the corral. Larry then climbed in to fondle the flowing mane and pat the lathered rump and mumble reassurances. After Stretch swung down, they relieved the animal of saddle and harness.

"While he's gentle, put him in another corral," Larry ordered Fat Pat and Elroy. "Either one of you can give him a rub down and some water soon as he's cool. Just keep talkin' friendly. I reckon he'll savvy." He patted Whitey again. "Gonna be a right smart saddler, this boy."

"What's ailin' you, young feller?" the ramrod demanded of Shorty, as the Texans quit the corral.

The runty cowhand had been petrified

during the invasion of the ranch-house porch by Toddy Allsop's startled horse. Rallying at last, a trifle on the pallid side, he now trudged across to where the deputy was conversing with the Frecker family.

"You'll be takin' your ladies to the social in your surrey, so I oughtn't ask if I can rent a buggy and come out here to drive Miss Desdemona," Shorty only half-heard Toddy's pitch. "But, by your leave, Mister Frecker, and if Miss Desdemona don't take it unkindly, I'd like to ask her to save a waltz for me."

"That's so *sweet*," giggled Lucy Lou.

"Hush your mouth, child," growled Dab. "Well, Desdemona?"

"Lands sakes," Addy said impatiently. "Mister Allsop's worthy enough, isn't he?"

"And — the way he protected us from that terrifying animal — was just wonderful!" enthused Lucy Lou.

"I must admit — I was most impressed," murmured Desdemona.

"It's possible I have underestimated you, Mister Allsop. And, of course . . . " She summoned up a gracious smile and fussed with her hair, "I'll certainly permit you to partner me in a waltz."

After making a mental note to have some obliging saloon bawd teach him to waltz, Toddy got down to official business, informing Dab he had been assigned by his superior to investigate last night's outrage. Dab promptly turned him over to the Texans and made to usher his womenfolk back into the house. It was then that the Frecker family became aware of the humble cowhand standing close to the porch, staring up at Lucy Lou.

"Somethin' fazin' you, boy?" Dab demanded. "I swear you look like you've seen a ghost."

"He's so pale," observed Addy.

"Cat got your tongue?" teased Lucy Lou.

Shorty found his voice then, but had difficulty in expressing his feelings.

"I froze — I just froze . . . " he

mumbled. "I turned round and looked and — Toddy's horse was on the porch and you — backed up against the rail. I was scared for you, Lucy Lou. I was so scared — I just froze."

He stared at the younger sister a long moment, then averted his gaze, mumbled something unintelligible and turned away. The Freckers stared after him, watching him trudge toward the bunkhouse, until Dab took his wife's arm. Desdemona followed her parents into the house and, a little while afterward, so did Lucy Lou; she had stayed out there, her eyes on Shorty Rudge, until he was lost from view.

After that set-to with the calico, Stretch felt the need to flop on his bunk a while.

"You don't need both of us along anyway," Larry told the deputy.

"Well, okay, but I have to . . . " began Toddy.

"Sure, you want to ask questions and see where it all happened," guessed

Larry. "Give me a minute to saddle a horse."

"It was Rudge sighted 'em first, right?" prodded Toddy. "I better talk to him while you're saddlin' up." As he headed that way, he traded waves with the cook unloading the wagon by his kitchen. "Howdy there, Roscoe! How ya been?"

"Same as always." Roscoe produced one of his rare grins. "Good to see you, Toddy."

In the bunkhouse, the deputy listened to Shorty's account of his run-in with the hooded riders. There wasn't much to tell, from the runty cowhand's point of view. He had been fazed by the raiders' guns and had taken cover. That was it.

Riding up the north slope with Larry a short time later he listened to a terse but detailed report of the incident. Larry pointed to the rock that had shielded Shorty and, from the rim, took the deputy on to the blackened, flattened area that had been thick with tinder-dry brush before being fired by the fleeing gunhawks.

He rolled and lit a cigarette and watched Toddy prowl the terrain west, well realizing this would provide no clue to the identity of the raiders nor the direction they had fled, but conceding Toddy's right to make a token effort. The deputy rode out of sight of him, returning some 15 minutes later to admit defeat.

"They left tracks sure enough, but I lost 'em on the rock flats yonder of the dry creek."

"So," said Larry, as they began their return to Circle 6, "nobody can prove they were Hammond riders. Not this time anyway."

"You said they wore hoods," Toddy reminded him. "We got to go by the rules, friend. You know how it is. Without some kind of proof, we can't . . ."

"You don't have to tell me," Larry said boredly.

"For a feller that near got himself

killed last night, you're plenty cool, seems to me," remarked Toddy. "And your buddy — breakin' that wild critter just now. Don't he have *no* nerves?"

"Man has a close shave, what's he supposed to do?" challenged Larry. "Sit around and fret about it for a week after?"

They made the rim and began the descent and, eyeing Larry covertly, Toddy began a fishing expedition.

"I bet them Frecker gals think you and Emerson're really somethin'."

"Relax," grinned Larry. "What they think don't bother us any. We ain't the marryin' kind, Deputy. So you get no competition from us."

"Just so everybody understands," muttered Toddy. "My intentions toward Miss Desdemona Frecker are strictly honorable."

"Yeah, sure," shrugged Larry.

"I'll tell you," confided Toddy. "Courtin' is a worrisome chore."

"I'll take your word for it," said Larry.

"But I ain't discouraged, on account of I got one thing goin' for me," Toddy assured him. "Desdemona took a shine to the other deputy, Grant Symes. Only Grant ain't interested, see? He's got his eye on Sheba Gilliam that runs the Jezebel Saloon."

"This is the courtin'est territory," mused Larry. "Every mother's son got the marryin' itch, it seems like."

Stretch was out of his bunk and straddling the top-rail of the corral now accommodating the calico, when Larry and the deputy returned. After offsaddling his horse, Larry climbed up there to join him. And now, as Roscoe emerged from his still to call an invitation to the deputy, Orv and the other hands watched in poker-faced anticipation.

"Like a shot to cheer you on your way, Toddy? Here's my best yet. The real good stuff!"

"I can't hardly wait," Toddy said, smacking his lips. "Best yet, huh Roscoe ol' pal?"

He dismounted, his eager eyes on the libation offered by his friend, a shot glass full. As he accepted the glass, Roscoe begged him.

"You don't just swig it down. First, you admire the color. Then you sniff the fine aroma."

"I'm lookin'. I'm sniffin'.'"

"Good whiskey got to be handled with respect, Toddy. Specially *my* stuff. This is no factory distilled rotgut. This is ambrosia."

"I can drink it now?"

"You can drink it now."

Toddy downed that shot in three measured gulps, smacked his lips again, rolled his eyes and, as he returned the empty glass, warmly congratulated Roscoe.

"Get to agree with you. That's the best yet."

"Great taste, huh?" bragged Roscoe, leering triumphantly at Orv and the hands. "Real smooth?"

"I never tasted better," declared Toddy. "And I sure thank you, Roscoe, but now I got to head back to town and write up my report."

The ramrod stayed impassive, but Fat Pat and his buddies were trading knowing grins and the Texans watching in keen interest as Toddy began remounting. At the third attempt, he managed to fit boot into stirrup. He then swung his other leg over, also the rest of him, and flopped to the dust to the other side.

"Clumsy," he chided himself.

Chagrined by the guffaws of the ranch-hands, Rosco chided the deputy.

"With a shot of my good liquor inside of you, you ought to be steady as a rock. C'mon now, Toddy. Show these jackasses how slick you can mount up and ride out."

"Well, sure," grinned Toddy. "Nothin' to it. Been gettin' on and off horses for years, haven't I?"

It took him 5 minutes, but he finally made it. Backside firmly planted in his saddle, boots snug in stirrups, he waved so-long and rode for the south slope.

"Looks like he's gonna be okay," observed the ramrod. "And that sure surprises me."

Toddy Allsop would make it back to town, the onlookers agreed. Eventually anyway. He parted company with his horse when it began climbing the upgrade, quickly remounted and fell only twice again before reaching the south rim and disappearing from view. By then, Fat Pat and Elroy were near hysterical and Orv aiming threatening scowls at the indignant Roscoe, who cussed the hands and assured Orv,

"This batch might just be a mite strong, but I can break it down some — with a little somethin' of my own."

"The day they hang you, it won't be for rustlin' nor for bank-robbin'," predicted Orv. "I'll be for poisonin' some poor bastard."

"I'll remember you for that, Orv Moran!" warned Roscoe.

"Some of these days I'm gonna fix me a firebrand," growled Orv. "I'll hurl it into your doggone still and blow the whole shebang sky-high."

"That's a helluva thing to say!" fumed Roscoe. "That's the most damn-awful thing you ever said to me, Orv Moran, and I won't forget it!"

Watching the cook trudge back to his still, Stretch grinned mildly and remarked to his partner, "Sure feels good. Back workin' on a good spread like Circle 6 I mean. After all our driftin' and outlaw-fightin' and riskin' our hides all the time. This is better for us, runt."

★ ★ ★

"Uh huh," grunted Larry. "Circle 6 is just right for us. We got a ramrod figures he's about ready for a rockin' chair, three spooked hired hands, a couple man-hungry females houndin' us, a chuck-boss that's likely stewin' locoweed into his moonshine booze and trigger-happy gunhawks that come raidin' regular. So what harm could happen to us on a spread like Circle 6?

147

It's our kind of ranch."

"I'm sure glad you feel that way," said Stretch, "on account of I like it here."

★ ★ ★

Mid-afternoon of that day, with the temperature still high, a Diamond H hand rode into Loomis to seek out the new doctor. Locals directed him to the modest house on Alliance Road where Oliver Jansen, his living quarters in order, his waiting room empty, sat alone in his kitchen and peeled potato; the new medico had not yet hired a housekeeper.

Spare of build, bespectacled and slightly stoop-shouldered, he presented that shaggy-haired, pre-occupied exterior typical of academics in the big universities back east. He had topped his class at medical school, graduating with high honors, and considered himself an efficient physician and a skilled surgeon, despite his self-effacing demeanor.

148

Talented he undoubtedly was, but short on personality.

The jangling of the doorbell was a cheering sound. He was only too willing to abandon the preparation of a lonely supper, don his alpaca coat and answer the call. The messenger informed him Miss Anna Hammond was poorly. Her brother, owner of the Diamond H ranch, would appreciate Doc Jansen's prompt attendance.

"Well, yes, certainly," nodded Jansen. "I suppose — uh — you'd have no knowledge of the lady's ailment?"

The cowhand wrinkled his brow.

"She faints a lot. Nobody told me, Doc. I heard Chloe — the housekeeper — say it once."

"I've not been to Diamond H before," said Jansen. "If you'll kindly direct me . . . "

"Northwest trail out of town," shrugged the cowhand. "How can you miss it? You pass Three Rocks, everything yonder is Hammond land. Mister Hammond says hustle, okay?"

"You may inform Mister Hammond I'm on my way," said Jansen. "I only have to harness my horse to my vehicle."

"I'll be headed back then," nodded the cowhand.

Summoned to attend the sister of the territory's wealthiest cattleman, the optimism of scholarly Dr Jansen was suddenly boosted.

"Definite step forward," he assured himself, while checking the contents of his valise. "Every new patient is welcome, even the lowliest, but the important people even more so. Fainting fits? Could be a variety of reasons. I wonder if the genial Doctor Conrad has ever attended the lady. Too bad I've no time to consult with him. Best get out there as quickly as possible."

To his credit, he made every effort to reach the Diamond H headquarters with all due speed. But he was still very much an easterner, out of his element here and overawed by Diamond H's vast holdings. He did take to the northwest trail, but became confused at the next crossroads beyond. A line-rider found him a half-hour later, took pity on him and steered him to a short-cut, but it was near sundown by the time he stalled his buggy in the broad patio fronting the imposing Hammond home. A servant directed him to the group seated on the porch, Hammond and sister, Howard Dortweil and Ed Rushford.

When he presented himself, the rancher studied him dubiously and remarked, "I hoped to welcome you sooner. Took you quite a time to get here."

"My apologies, Mister Hammond. I do have an excuse — which must seem rather feeble to you. I'm afraid I lost my way."

Hammond shrugged resignedly and performed introductions, after which Dortweil smiled blandly and chided Jansen for his tardiness. Anna, he pointed out, had revived two hours ago and was feeling much better now.

"Much better, Doctor," Anna assured him.

"But you've fainted before?" asked Jansen.

"It happens too often for my liking," declared Hammond. "Now that you've finally arrived, maybe you can find out just what's the matter with her."

"I'm sure it's nothing serious, Kyle," said Anna.

"I certainly hope not, but let's give Doctor Jansen a chance to diagnose . . ." Hammond shrugged irritably, "whatever it is."

"Oh, very well," said Anna, rising. "If you're so concerned."

"No more than I, my dear Anna," said Dortweil. "Your welfare is my constant preoccupation." He nodded courteously to the medico. "Only your best efforts on Anna's behalf, if you please."

"Yes, of course," frowned Jansen.

"Go on, Sis," urged Hammond.

"Have Chloe take Doctor Jansen to your room. Let's try and get to the cause of your swooning once and for all."

After Anna had taken the doctor inside, the men resumed their interrupted conversation.

"Digging for water is not the answer, you were saying," Dortweil reminded Rushford.

"I go along with Mister Hammond," said Rushford. "In this part of the county, we have to count on enough rain to keep the feed-grass growin'. No water underground. Not enough of it anyway."

"The only solution to the immediate problem is Sun Basin," Hammond said flatly. "Frecker has more water than he needs. One way or another, he has to co-operate."

"Stubborn old sonofagun, Frecker," remarked Rushford.

"And you'll resort to harsh measures if all else fails, Kyle," said Dortweil. "Ruthless when needs be? I admire you for that. You can't be swayed by sentiment in a crisis of such magnitude."

"Even so, don't get the idea I enjoy harassing Frecker," muttered the rancher. "I have power, Howard. I guess I throw a bigger shadow than any citizen of this country. But power is something you have to know how to handle. I'm an impatient man. Yes, ruthless too. And — right now — I'm also becoming desperate. Power and desperation, Howard. Bad combination. So this is no time for losing my head."

"Guess I'd best choose nighthawks now," drawled Rushford, getting to his feet.

"Tell them to stay sharp, Ed," ordered Hammond. "The shape the herd's in, we can't risk a stampede."

For Jansen, his examination of his new patient, his questions and her clear answers, became an unsettling experience. Try as he might, he could not yet diagnose her problem. To make it worse, he was inept at hiding his confusion.

"You're making me feel quite guilty, Doctor." In cheerful mood she challenged him. "I'm a puzzle to you, am I not?"

"Well," he shrugged. "Not all ailments can be quickly diagnosed."

Their conversation continued while, behind a screen and with the house-keeper's assistance, she redonned her clothing. At the table near the bedroom doorway, he replaced his stethoscope in his bag and did some deep thinking.

"I'm afraid being a difficult patient will be a new experience for me, Doctor. I may even develop a guilt complex."

That last remark impressed him.

"Complex," he repeated. "One does not expect to hear such a word used in a frontier community — and correctly. It is obvious, Miss Anna, you've had the benefit of a good education."

"Marbrow College, Baltimore," she offered.

"Remarkable coincidence," he frowned.

"A patient I attended yesterday, a small boy who fell and gashed an arm, his mother is an alumna of Marbrow."

"Oh, you'd have to mean my dear friend Dorrie McQueen."

"Yes, that's the name."

"We went to Marbrow together and were room-mates, graduated together. Been friends a long time, went to the local school when we were just children."

A few minutes later, emerging from behind the screen, she dismissed the housekeeper, took his arm and made to usher him from the room. It was then that he chanced to glance toward the framed photograph on her dressing table. A theory was building in his mind; the case might prove not quite as complicated as he had feared.

"May I enquire — is that a picture of your parents?"

"Why, yes," she nodded. "As a matter of fact, the last photograph ever taken of them. Of course we have others."

"May I see the picture?"

"If you wish." Watching him move across to study the photograph, she smiled indulgently and hazarded a guess.

"You have a keen interest in old photographs?"

"The subjects, rather than the photography," he muttered. "Do you have others?"

"Other photographs?"

"Of your parents. If it wouldn't be too much trouble . . . "

"Not at all, Doctor, but I don't understand . . . "

"I am developing a theory, Miss Anna."

For another ten minutes, the patient fossicked in the bottom drawer of a bureau, bringing to light other pictures of her long-dead parents. And, during this, she found herself answering more questions. Why was he so interested in her grandparents, on both sides of the family? He had his reasons, he assured her.

Later, when they rejoined Hammond and Dortweil, the rancher announced it was now suppertime.

"Can't send you home hungry, Doctor. Why don't you stay and . . . ?"

"I shouldn't impose," Jansen said apologetically. "On the other hand, I've not fully completed my investigation of Miss Anna's condition. It's possible I'll have more questions . . . "

"More questions?" she asked incredulously. "Really, Doctor, there can't be much else you'd need to know about me."

"Just a few more details," he frowned.

"Come on now," growled Hammond. "Do you know what's wrong with my sister or don't you?"

"Surely, by now, you have *some* idea?" challenged Dortweil.

"Excuse me, Mister Dortweil," said the medico. "I need a little more time for . . . "

"Doctor Jansen is developing a theory," interjected Anna.

"What use are theories?" demanded

Hammond. "Find the cause, then treat it — and quickly."

"That is my intention, Mister Hammond," Jansen assured him. "And now . . . " He offered a hesitant smile, "I'm suddenly quite hungry and you've been kind enough to invite me to dine with you."

"You have to excuse my impatience," sighed Hammond, as they made their way to the dining room. "As you can see, I'm not exactly puny, haven't had a day's sickness since I can't remember when. So, naturally, with Anna so frail all the time, I worry about her, wonder how and why."

"I do understand," said Jansen.

"Mister Dortweil is her fiance, you see," explained Hammond. "He's devoted to her, I'm sure, but I can't help wondering if a woman in her condition is ready for marriage. I've said it before and I'll say it again. She faints too often."

Over supper in the territory's most richly appointed dining room, the young physician listened politely to his host's dissertation on the drought threatening the local economy, but refrained from comment. As well as enjoying an excellent meal, he was keeping an eye on his patient and secretly congratulating himself.

"She gave me the clue without realizing it," he reflected. "What an opportune time for her to use the word — complex. It's all so clear now. I'm right. I just *know* I'm right."

To Dortweil's annoyance, Jansen asked to speak privately with Anna after supper. Hammond was again becoming exasperated, but the medico had his way. His sister conducted Jansen to a ground floor parlor while, with Dortweil, he strolled out to the front porch. They settled into comfortable chairs, lit cigars, and then Dortweil sourly remarked, "I don't trust that fellow."

6

A Night To Remember

THE master of Diamond H crossed his long legs and slanted a glance to his guest's handsome profile.

"He's a qualified physician, obviously," he frowned. "There'd have to be the customary diploma on view in his waiting room. Chances of some charlatan masquerading as a doctor in this territory are remote, Howard. Their bona fides are too easily checked."

"I wasn't referring to his professional qualifications," said Dortweil.

"What then?" demanded Hammond.

"Doesn't it strike you he's taking a personal interest in Anna?" challenged Dortweil.

Hammond chuckled good-humoredly. "Damn it, Howard, you're jealous!"

"Cautious," countered Dortweil. "And always preoccupied with Anna's welfare."

"Jansen isn't competition," scoffed Hammond. "I never heard anything so ridiculous. As if Anna would spare a thought for a man as dull as Jansen, a plodding bachelor fresh out of medical school. Compared to you, Howard, he's downright nondescript."

"Well, he'd better be skilled at his profession," declared Dortweil. "That's a precious patient he's attending, Kyle."

Seated on the parlor sofa, watching the young doctor pace back and forth, Anna was protesting,

"I don't understand this new line of questioning."

"If you'll answer the questions frankly," said Jansen, "I believe we'll reach a solution, Miss Anna."

"Oh, very well," she shrugged. "I admit I was somewhat startled at the change in Dorrie McQueen. From the time we graduated, she's become so — so . . ."

"The lady is overweight," he said

162

bluntly. "Go on, please."

"I remember thinking — how terrible it would be . . . "

"If the same thing happened to you?"

"This is becoming embarrassing, Doctor. It's as though you're reading my mind."

"In a way, yes. But with your best interests at heart."

"All right, I couldn't bear the thought of becoming the fat lady of Diamond H. I promised myself I'd avoid overeating."

"And your meal this evening . . . " He paused to eye her intently. "That was, for you, a typical supper?"

"Yes," she nodded. "Why?"

"Miss Anna, I have only one criticism of your eating routine," he said earnestly. "The meal was excellent, cooked to perfection and very nourishing. But your portion was too little. You simply don't eat as much as you should. The idea of not overeating makes good sense. But — forgive me — you've taken it to extremes. And the pity of it is your chances of ever becoming

163

obese are very slight indeed. Perhaps you now understand my interest in the pictures of your forebears. Your parents were trim-figured — when well past middle-age. There is no hereditary obesity in your family."

"I'm beginning to feel — very foolish," she murmured. "Doctor, you're saying I'm under-nourished? It's malnutrition that causes my fainting spells?" As he averted his gaze, she said firmly, "*Your* turn to be frank, Doctor."

"You don't have anaemia, I'm glad to say. And the cure? Surely you've guessed."

"I should eat more." She smiled self-consciously. "Because I don't have to worry about becoming — like Dorrie."

"Within a week, you'll feel stronger," he promised. "The lethargy will leave you. You'll have more energy. Your color will improve and, unless you're subject to sudden shocks, the fainting spells will pass. You don't need medicine, Miss Anna. All you need is normal nourishment."

"I'm most grateful to you, Doctor," she murmured, rising, offering her hand. "How intuitive you are, and so very wise — for so young a physician."

To her amusement, Jansen was suddenly red-faced.

"Very — uh — kind of you to say so," he mumbled.

"I'm impressed," she smiled. "And I look forward to seeing you at the Saturday social. Of course I'll save you a dance."

"I'll not be there," he sighed. After holding her hand a moment, he released it. "I too have my complex. I'm inclined to be clumsy in some ways. Never could learn to dance. Bad co-ordination, I'm afraid."

"What a pity," she frowned.

In the front hall, he retrieved his hat and bag. She ushered him out to the porch and, at once, her brother demanded to be told,

"Have you finally diagnosed the condition?"

"And recommended the remedy,

165

Mister Hammond," nodded Jansen. "I have to get back to town now. If you have questions, Miss Anna will answer them I'm sure, since the condition is not of a too personal nature." He bowed to them. "Miss Anna, Mister Hammond, Mister Dortweil, it's been a pleasure. And thank you for a fine supper."

"You're welcome," frowned Hammond. "I thank you for — whatever you've done for Anna." He studied his sister's smiling face a moment, then watched the medico descend to his rig. When the buggy was rolling away from the ranch-house, he eyed Anna again. "You're really satisfied?"

"Very much so," she declared.

"Good," he nodded. "When he gets around to sending his bill, I'll pay promptly, and with pleasure."

"You seem more relaxed now, my dear," observed Dortweil.

"I suppose it was preying on my mind," she said, as he helped her into a chair. "Well, the patient is much relieved, having been assured her condition is curable."

"You don't have to talk about it if you'd rather not," said Hammond.

"And I'd rather not," she said ruefully. "Let's spare my feelings for the time being, Kyle. Later, perhaps I'll explain it to you."

"In your own good time," he shrugged.

"That scruffy doctor-fellow caused you embarrassment?" challenged Dortweil. "The nerve of him!"

"No, Howard," she protested. "He could not have been more considerate. Why, he's the kindest, gentlest . . ."

"If he's good at his work, that's all that matters," opined Hammond.

Dr Oliver Jansen, the odd man out of Loomis County, should have felt easier of mind while driving homeward. By applying simple psychology and using his powers of observation, he had solved what might have become a quite critical case; a few more months of under-nourishment and Miss Anna Hammond would have become a cot case. Why this disquiet assailing him now? He wasn't feeling at all pleased with himself, despite his successful investigation of the patient's problem. The lady had been foolish, but he wasn't considering that aspect.

"Your problem," he chided himself, "is your too personal interest. You've broken the medico's golden rule, Oliver. Instead of holding yourself aloof, maintaining a strictly professional attitude, you are indulging yourself in a personal concern for the lady's well-being — and for her future happiness. Admit it, Oliver. You're jealous of that Dortweil fellow. You actually dislike the man, and for no valid reason. Unforgiveable, Oliver. And very unprofessional."

★ ★ ★

By Saturday afternoon, all interested parties were caught up in preparations for the big social event scheduled to begin at 8 p.m. in the town hall.

In conference with his aides, Sheriff Phil Tarren decided both deputies should attend the function.

"You'll be responsible for keepin' the affair goin' in an orderly fashion," he sternly announced. "That means you'll wear your badges of office and you'll be the only guests packin' sidearms. Grant, you're in charge of relievin' all males of their hardware at the front door. There'll be a rack for hangin' gunbelts and you'll be supplied with tags for identifyin' each hogleg."

"Whatever you say, Phil," nodded Symes. "I figure I'll still get my chance to dance with Sheba."

"She's gonna be there?" Tarren asked dubiously.

"Along with some of her girls." Symes was suddenly on the defensive. "And why not, might I ask? That's a saloon she operates, Phil. Not a whore-house."

"Well, there'll be other saloonkeepers attendin'," offered Toddy. "So why not Sheba Gilliam?"

169

"It don't matter to me," Tarren hastened to assure Symes. "But some of our high-falutin' female citizens, such as the Reverend's wife and sister and Mrs Mayor Appleton and Doc Conrad's wife, well now, they're apt to look down their noses, know what I mean?"

"Let 'em," shrugged Symes.

"Toddy, you'll keep circulatin'," said Tarren. "I'm lookin' to you to keep an eye on the refreshment supplied by the Reverend's womenfolk and their friends — them other old killjoy biddies. We don't want no smart-aleck spikin' the punch bowls with hard liquor. That kind of foolery I won't abide, savvy?"

"I'll keep my eyes peeled," said Toddy.

"You'll also keep an eye on our local riff-raff," said Tarren. "No wild dancin', no rough stuff, no loud talk and no cussin'. You got that?"

"I got it," nodded Toddy.

The sheriff mopped his sweaty brow and expressed a sentiment shared by the whole county.

"This'd be a *real* celebration, a night to remember, the best ever, if it started rainin' right now."

Out at Circle 6, Dab Frecker was gratified to learn there would be only one of his employees absenting himself from the affair; only Roscoe Cully, that anti-social misfit, was staying home tonight. Dab and his foreman traded many a conspiratorial grin from 5 p.m. onward. They shared a secret that caused them some degree of smug satisfaction. Each would be equipped with a pint of good rye whiskey, these items being concealed on their persons when they entered the hall. As they had done on other such social occasions, they would empty those bottles into the punch bowls at their first opportunity, thus ensuring the non-alcoholic refreshment supplied by Loomis's temperance faction would be fit to be imbibed by cattlemen.

Dab would not have been so gratified had he known of the cook's furtive achievement an hour earlier. Toting a quart jug of his latest concoction, Roscoe had sneaked into the bunkhouse and found it temporarily deserted. He had also found Orv's bottle. The contents thereof had been poured out the rear window and the bottle refilled from Roscoe's jug and carefully re-stoppered.

Gaining entry to the master bedroom of the ranch-house was an even greater achievement; except for the foreman, no Circle 6 man dared cross the threshold of the front door, let alone place a ladder against a wall and climb to a second floor window. Dab's bottle was hidden from his wife's prying eyes, but Roscoe, a dedicated hunter, rooted it out and repeated his routine of substituting his moonshine booze for high grade rye.

Larry and Stretch were glad to see their bunkhouse buddies rubbing dubbin into boots and taking an all-over bath, looking out their best duds in expectation of making a favorable impression on the ladies of Loomis. Fat Pat, Shorty and Elroy were accompanying the Freckers to the festivities, but only because they were relying on the new hands to block any rough stuff attempted by Diamond H men. And, to the Texans, this was a saddening thought.

Larry put his thoughts into words, but was cheerfully assured by his partner,

"Their time'll come one of these days. Somethin'll happen. Their gizzard'll be put to the test and they won't be found wantin'."

At the time prescribed by Dab, Orv and the hands mounted up and flanked the Frecker surrey. Dab drove the rig out of the basin proudly, his younger daughter perched beside him, her mother and sister sharing the rear seat, the better to prevent creasing of their ball gowns. In new shirts and pants and clean-shaven, the Texans figured they'd done their best to appear presentable.

Circle 6 and the Diamond H force reached the town hall at about the same time. Though Kyle Hammond spared Dab only a curt nod, Dab doffed his hat and aimed a paternal, approving smile at the winsome Anna and her impeccably tailored suitor.

Sheriff Tarren was patrolling the opposite sidewalk and trading pleasantries with townfolk converging on the hall, which soon began filling. Deputies Symes and Allsop were already on duty inside, Symes checking pistols, his colleague striving to keep several areas under surveillance at the same time. Twice, he had failed to detect the surreptitious spiking of the punch bowls on the white-covered tables by the northside wall of the gaily-festooned dance floor. Several townmen had succeeded in boosting the punch before Dab and Orv did likewise.

There was much preliminary socializing in the now crowded hall, Hammond introducing the visiting "financier" to various of his leading citizens, Larry and Stretch renewing acquaintance with bar-owner Tim Doherty, who introduced them to a laughing-eyed brunette in bright green satin.

"This is one night I don't mind mixin' with my competition," grinned the jovial Doherty. "Boys, say howdy to Trottie Locke, one of Sheba Gilliam's girls. You likely heard of Sheba. Runs the Jezebel, couple blocks down from my place?"

Trottie started in flirting rightaway, despite having difficulty deciding which Texan she preferred, the deep-voiced one with the muscles and the genial grin or the beanpole with the sheepish grin. This might have developed into a triangle situation, had the musicians not arrived at that moment. Being volunteers, these five obliging locals were smiled upon by people eager to begin dancing.

Two of the musicians, one toting a guitar, the other a fiddle, quenched their thirsts from a punch bowl before taking their positions on the dais. A few moments later, just as the cornetist was about to announce the first dance, the guitarist and the fiddler fell off their chairs and were carried from the hall by solicitous friends. Dr Will Conrad hurried after them, after complaining to his spouse,

"Some joker's done it again."

"Done what again, Will?"

"Never mind, Harriet. Just stay clear of the punch."

The dismay of the surviving musicians and the impatience of the would-be dancers gave Larry and Stretch their best chance of parting company with tenacious Trottie Locke.

"'Scuse us, ma'am," Stretch mumbled gratefully. "Seems like my friend and me gonna have to help out here."

To the keen approval of the Freckers, the Texans made their way to the dais. Larry picked up the fallen guitar, Stretch the fiddle and bow and nodded reassuringly to the man with the cornet.

"Get to tootin'," Larry urged him. "Any tune you fancy."

"You gents read music?" asked the orchestra leader.

"Just trail-sign," said Larry.

"A newspaper once in a while," offered Stretch.

"Maybe a Sears Roebuck catalog," said Larry.

"Just so long as you ain't professional," muttered the cornetist. "We don't read music neither. So let's just play. Everybody know 'Pretty Ella May'?" He waved to the crowd. "Gents, choose your partners and *here we go* . . . !"

He began tootling the well-known melody with the flute and trombone joining in and, after the first few bars, the trouble-shooters were strumming and fiddling right along. The dancing got under way, all eyes on the fashionably-gowned Anna and her urbane partner. That first lively tune was followed by a waltz, thus providing the Freckers with the opportunity of dancing together; Dab was good only for waltzing.

Shorty Rudge now partnered Lucy

Lou, relishing her proximity and going to pains to avoid stepping on her dainty feet.

Among the crowd, Diamond H men ignored Shorty and his colleagues and fixed narrowed eyes on the substitute musicians.

"Big jasper with the guitar," Burt Marcus whispered to one of his cohorts. "He's the one near tore my head off with a rifle-slug. Skinny bastard with the fiddle — he'd be his side-kick."

"So all we got to do is wait," muttered the other man. "We'll get our chance, Burt. Count on it."

Between dances, chatting with Anna and some of her friends, Dortweil chanced to glance toward the entrance. The somewhat voluptuous Sheba Gilliam, proprietress of the Jezebel Saloon, was bedecked in a figure-hugging gown of deep blue to compliment her glowing blonde hair, laughing indulgently at this moment, ear cocked to a drawled compliment from Grant Symes. She was side-on to Dortweil, not looking his way; for this he was abjectly grateful.

He begged to be excused and began seeking Rushford, all the time keeping his face averted from the blonde woman over by the main entrance. The musicians were performing again. One of Sheba Gilliam's regulars requested the pleasure and, watched yearningly by Symes, they joined the dancers. It was then that Dortweil sighted Rushford in conversation with a couple of townmen. His urgent signal brought Rushford to his side.

"You look like hell," chided Rushford, noting his haunted expression. "Damn it, you're supposed to be the cool dude from back east. What're you frettin' about?"

"I'll keep my back to the dancers," muttered Dortweil. "You keep your eyes peeled for a blonde woman in a dark blue gown. She's being partnered by a heavyset jasper."

"What woman?"

"Blonde I said! Blonde and flashy.

A minute ago she was talking to a deputy."

"Oh, to Symes? Sure, I saw her too. Mighty well-known in Loomis. Owns the Jezebel Saloon. So?"

"Ed, *she* knows *me*! Her name's Gilliam, and . . . !"

"That's the name. Sheba Gilliam. What about her?"

"Let's get out of here. This has to be said in private."

The night was becoming warmer and quite a few locals quitting the hall to take the air below the town hall steps. Dortweil and Rushford made their exit casually, lit cigars and withdrew out of earshot.

"All right," frowned Rushford. "Let's hear it."

"The Gilliam woman could foul up our whole deal," declared Dortweil. "She only has to catch sight of me, Ed. That's all it would take. She'd scream thief, run to the law — and I'd be finished."

"You that sure she'd remember you?"

180

demanded Rushford.

"It wasn't that long ago," scowled Dortweil. "Less than two years. Belvort, Missouri."

"You were workin' a bunko operation," guessed Rushford.

"Skinned quite a few suckers in that town, and she was one of them," said Dortweil. "She'd remember me for sure, Ed. Of all the lousy luck. Our big chance to set ourselves up for life, and she has to be here in Loomis."

"And not just passin' through," said Rushford. "She's here to stay."

"We don't have cash enough to buy her off," fretted Dortweil.

"The hell with that," growled Rushford. "A woman like her? Forget it. If she got wise to our deal, she wouldn't settle for just one handout. She'd get greedy."

"Something has to be done," insisted Dortweil.

"That'll be my chore," said Rushford. "Somebody has to shut her mouth, and it better be me. I'll take care of it when

181

this shindig breaks up. Meanwhile, you tread wary, boy. Make damn sure she don't spot you."

"The Hammonds will wonder what became of me," frowned Dortweil. "But that's okay. I'll think up some excuse."

After another hour of playing for the seemingly tireless crowd, the musicians needed a break, and that went double for the volunteer guitarist and fiddler, both craving to smoke. The leader announced a 10-minute interval and, trading grins, the tall man descended from the dais and fished out their makings. On this very sociable occasion, they didn't mind helping out in the band; they were enjoying themselves.

"No offense," drawled Larry. "But, when it comes to fiddlin', you're some helluva horse-breaker."

"You're doin' just fine, runt," grinned Stretch. "On account of nobody's noticed that guitar is out of tune."

"Includin' me," Larry confessed.

To date, the festivities had been

unmarred by rowdyism. There had, however, been several unfortunate incidents. Mrs Pickard, the preacher's wife, seemed to undergo some kind of personality change after a few sips of punch. Her husband, a quick thinker in time of crisis, forestalled her attempt to dance solo and discreetly spirited her away. The wife of the mayor, who had accounted for one whole glass of punch, suffered a giggling fit and was attempting to seduce the local Western Union operator when, to that citizen's alarm, she passed out and collapsed at his feet. Old Jordy Carew, rheumaticky and a widower these past 20 years, experienced temporary rejuvenation after his second visit to the refreshment tables. As well as challenging blacksmith Bull Baisley to a wrestling contest and trying to pick a fight with Tim Doherty, he startled several ladies by pinching vulnerable sections of their anatomy.

The Texans had rolled cigarettes and were fishing for matches when a burly local nudged Stretch and, with an amiable grin, restrained them from lighting up.

"No smokin' inside the hall, boys. Special request from the ladies, you know? Any gent craves a smoke, he goes out back. Come on, I'll show you the way. Feel like a smoke myself."

"Why, sure," shrugged Stretch.

"Yeah, let's not offend the ladies," said Larry.

Shorty Rudge, sighting the trio making for the rear exit, nervously remarked to Fat Pat,

"That's a Diamond H man with Larry and Stretch."

"Damned if it ain't," frowned Fat Pat.

"And I saw a half-dozen of Hammond's crew sneak out back a couple minutes ago," said Shorty. "Hey, Pat, I'm gettin' a bad feelin' in my gut."

"Me too." Fat Pat shrugged uncomfortably. "But, hell, it ain't none of our business."

"Least we could do is take a look,"

Shorty suggested.

"Well, all right then," mumbled Fat Pat. "But, if there's gonna be any rough stuff, all I'm gonna do is look. I don't crave to get beat up."

The well-lit area behind the town hall, a great deal of open ground, didn't have the look of a potential arena. A dozen or so men were out there, smoking, talking among themselves, when the Texans appeared, relaxed, unsuspecting.

Then, with startling suddenness, their burly escort got behind Stretch and swung a hard fist to the back of his neck. Stretch made a gasping sound and began sagging and Larry too was taken by surprise; three men rushed him, pounding at him. He barely had time to recognize one of his adversaries of Farley Creek before his legs were kicked from under him.

Non-combatants had promptly hurried across to block the rear exit against interference from either deputy. From their point of view, an all-in brawl was greater entertainment than dancing. Shorty and Fat Pat, jostled by the excited onlookers, peered apprehensively at the scene of mayhem.

Stretch was upright now, but with two Diamond H men gripping his arms and a third raining blows at him. While the Circle 6 boys watched, the taller Texan lunged back against his captors and swung a belly-kick that sent his assailant reeling. Still down, Larry was rolling, desperate to escape the savage kicks aimed at him by two attackers, one of them the wild-eyed Burt Marcus. Half-rising, he caught a swinging boot, gripped it hard and twisted, bringing Marcus down. He was struggling to his feet when Diamond H reinforcements came to the fore; three descended on him, arms flailing.

"Aw, hell," groaned Fat Pat.

"Don't you wish . . . " Shorty grimaced in disgust, "don't you wish you had nerve enough?"

"There's too many of 'em," fretted Fat Pat.

"Uh huh," grunted Orv. He startled them by clamping hands to their shoulders as he stared into the yard. "Too many for Larry and Stretch to handle. But they ain't quittin'."

Elroy Hagenthorpe had tagged the ramrod through the rear doorway. Now, he wished he hadn't. The fury of the fracas made his gorge rise. Larry had felled one assailant and was grappling with another when a third leapt at him from behind, locking an arm about his neck. Stretch's captors still had his arms imprisoned; he was again taking punishment, but not flinching, just cussing, lashing out at his attackers with his boots.

"I'm too old to get into this," Orv said dolefully. "And you young bucks ain't got the gizzard. Seems an awful shame, huh?"

Larry went down again, taking two adversaries with him in a wildly struggling heap, while other Diamond H men hovered close, waiting their chance to get at him. Stretch kicked the shin of his attacker and, as the man wailed and bowed over, brought a knee up and caught him on the chin.

Something happened to Shorty then. He suddenly realized he couldn't do it, couldn't just stand and watch the defiant Texans worn down by force of numbers.

"The hell with 'em!" he gasped.

And, as he charged into the fray, Fat Pat found the courage to barge after him. Elroy was horrified, fearful of what might happen to his bunkhouse buddies, but unable to shift his gaze.

The preliminary efforts of Shorty and Fat Pat were inept. More by luck than skill, they lent aid to the almost overpowered Texans. Shorty, confronting a man about to aim a kick at the prone Larry, did some hard kicking on his own account. The Hammond waddy swore luridly as the runty cowpoke's boot slammed at his shinbone. He was hopping on one foot when Shorty swung wildly with his bunched right. Being a full 8 inches shorter than the other man, he missed his target, the unprotected chin, and struck lower, right to the Adam's apple. The lurid profanity was choked off; the man crumpled. During this, Fat Pat was dodging to avoid punishment from a Diamond H man, dodging so frantically that he overbalanced. Right beside the chubby cowhand, another Hammond man was half-prone, about to rise, when the full weight of Fat Pat descended on his head and shoulders. His face was rammed into the ground with devastating impact. He was still prone, out cold, by the time Fat Pat made it to his feet.

Shorty flung himself at the men grasping Stretch's arms. He grasped an ear and twisted it, rammed an elbow into the other man's ribs and, conscious of the weakening grips, Stretch shook free, loosed a rebel yell and began retaliating in spectacular style. Larry and his assailants were lurching upright again when Fat Pat joined that struggling foursome. He hooked an arm about a neck and, as a hand was shoved into his face, opened his mouth, got part of that paw between his teeth and bit hard. Suddenly less encumbered, Larry growled ferociously. He'd had his fill of defending himself; now he attacked — fiercely.

"I'm too old and you're too afeared, boy," Orv droned at Elroy, as he moved forward. "But I don't see how we can stay out of this."

"Well — uh — . . . " began Elroy.

"Take this and use it," ordered Orv. He had hustled Elroy to the woodheap behind the hall and seized a 3-foot length. Elroy accepted it. Orv armed himself with another such makeshift club. "Well? What're we waitin' for?"

Though reinforced, the Texans' first attackers were very soon getting the worst of that hectic set-to. The onlookers blocking the rear exit cheered excitedly, closing ranks as Toddy Allsop tried to force his way through to the scene of conflict. Battered, in pain but undaunted, the Texans were wreaking

190

vengeance, Larry bobbing and weaving, inflicting heavy punishment on every Diamond H man in reach of his rock-hard fist. The punch he landed on Marcus sent that rogue spinning to the dust. Another loomed before him and stopped an uppercut that lifted and deposited him atop Marcus. Stretch seemed to be in several places at one time. He moved so fast the onlookers weren't able to follow his actions, charging his adversaries, hitting them with everything, seizing one bodily and heaving him all the way to the woodheap, while Shorty and Fat Pat slugged it out gamely with cursing hard cases and Orv and Elroy finished off others with their improvised clubs; every man they clobbered went down and stayed down.

By the time Toddy managed to barge through the laughing crowd, the dust was settling; the only men still on their feet were the Circle 6 half-dozen. In varying stages of unconsciousness, eight Diamond H men littered the area. There were other Hammond men on hand, but now they were holding back, intimidated by the durability of two Texans and the new-found fighting spirit of Orv and the younger cowhands. Shorty, Fat Pat and Elroy were wildeyed and winded, but not about to quit.

"Great — sufferin' — Sadie!" gasped the deputy.

"Little private ruckus, Toddy," drawled Orv, discarding his club. "All over now. No call for the law to buy in."

"Yeah . . . " Larry blew on his knuckles and traded wry grins with Stretch. "All over now."

"We'd best get away from here," muttered Orv. "Get your boys cleaned up. Can't have you escortin' the family home — lookin' like you been in a fight."

"Well, hell, no," chuckled Stretch.

"The well back of Ogilvie's Barn," said Orv, turning away. "Follow me, if you can still walk."

"We can still walk," Shorty mumbled through puffed lips. "Takes more'n a bunch of Diamond H waddies to lick *us*."

7

Texas Tag-Along

WORKING the handle of the windlass a short time later, Larry winced. The victorious Circle 6 crew had followed their ramrod to the cluttered yard behind a livery stable and now craved the feel of cold water on their hot and bruised faces. Hauling up that first brimming pail, Larry felt his arm muscles ache, his bruised ribs smarting a protest. This time, he had taken quite a battering. So had Stretch. But, right now, the veteran trouble-shooters weren't about to complain. Something pretty damn wonderful had happened to their young colleagues this night; they were mutually agreed they had set an example and should take credit.

The triumphant warriors took turns

to swab blood and grime from their faces and dusted themselves off as best they could, while Orv solemnly reverted to his old man outlook.

"That ruckus was just too much for a man of my years," he intoned. "I give thanks I didn't suffer some kind of seizure. Thought sure my heart'd quit on me."

"You're still plenty spry, Orv," Stretch cheerfully assured him. "You did just fine."

"You hombres too," said Larry, aiming a companionable grin at the younger men. "The beanpole and me, we're right obliged."

"By golly we are," nodded Stretch. "As I recall, you busted into that hassle at just the right time."

"Of course — uh — that's what we expected," lied Larry. "We knew, soon as you saw what was happenin', you'd just naturally jump in and help us out."

"Hey, we did good, huh?" enthused Fat Pat. "Didn't we give 'em hell — didn't we?"

"First big Diamond H bastard I hit, he sure felt it," muttered Shorty. "Up till then, I was more spooked than mad. From then on till it ended, I wasn't spooked at all. Just stayed mad and kept right on swingin'."

"All it takes to settle their hash is a rap on their dumb heads with a good-sized hunk of firewood," bragged Elroy. "You want to know how I feel. Ashamed of ever fearin' Diamond H."

"Next time I'm nighthawkin', the Lord help any Diamond H hotshots come a'raidin'," chuckled Fat Pat. "I'll be ready for 'em with that ol' forty-five of mine. Might borrow me Roscoe's scattergun too. Hot damn! I could take on the whole Hammond outfit!"

"I'd as soon be their friend than their enemy," declared Shorty. "But, if fightin's what they want, fightin's what they'll get."

"Now you're talkin'," growled Elroy. "We got gizzard. We're an outfit now."

"That's it," Larry said approvingly. "You're the Circle 6 bunch. You don't back down."

"Time's gettin' on," drawled Orv, staring away toward the town hall. "The way we look, we oughtn't show our faces inside. I'm still passable respectable, so I'll go collect our hardware. And then we better wait by the rig for the folks."

Around midnight, when the Reverend Pickard reminded the revelers he would be expecting them for Sunday services, the function began breaking up. It was then that Dortweil rejoined the Hammonds and offered apologies for his prolonged absence.

"Must say I feel downright foolish about it," he muttered. "The simple truth is, I became rather ill, had to get away from the hall."

"The punch," scowled Hammond. "Let's be grateful Anna didn't try it. I'm pretty sure some idiot spiked it."

"Some westerner's idea of a practical joke, no doubt," remarked Dortweil. "Anna, my dear, you do look tired."

"I enjoyed myself," she smiled. "But

you're right, Howard. I am a little tired, so . . . ?"

"Time we were headed home," said Hammond.

For his murderous purpose, Ed Rushford had chosen what seemed the ideal vantagepoint. The alleymouth on Main Street's east side was a block down from the town hall and the Jezebel Saloon further south. He had only to wait for Sheba Gilliam to pass by; with less than two blocks to travel, she was hardly likely to be using a vehicle of any kind.

The blonde woman was still in festive mood and would have been one of the last to leave the hall but for the indisposition suffered by a friend and employee. Trottie Locke had unwisely accounted for a glass and a half of punch and was now in a reduced condition, dazed and mumbling and less than steady on her feet. And so, when Sheba quit the hall to begin the short walk to the Jezebel, she was good-humoredly supporting the younger woman.

"Let that be a lesson, Trottie honey," she chuckled. "The booze at a church social's liable to be heftier than what we sell at the saloon, specially if a sport or two gave it a jolt."

"I never — tasted anything like it!" groaned Trottie.

"Them that spiked the punch weren't all whiskey drinkers," guessed Sheba. "Might've been rum in it. Brandy too. And gin."

"Oh, Lawd," sighed Trottie. "Don't let's talk of it!"

A short distance from the hall, Sheba glanced over her shoulder at the people making ready for their homeward journey. Kyle Hammond was on the seat of his handsome surrey and his sister being helped into the vehicle by his guest. The Frecker surrey was stalled on the other side of the street, Larry and Stretch helping Dab's womenfolk aboard, Dab climbing to the driver's seat, Orv and the other hands already mounted. She ignored

199

the Circle 6 people. Freezing in her tracks with Trottie slumped against her, she stared hard at the courtly newcomer attending Anna Hammond.

"Could we get on home, Sheba — *please* . . . ?" pleaded Trottie.

"That cheatin' dude!" scowled Sheba. "It's *him*! I'd know him anywhere!"

"I'm gonna be sick again," complained Trottie.

"All right, all right," nodded Sheba. "I'll bed you down. And then I'll take care of that welsher."

Recognizing the taller of the two women, Rushford drew and cocked his six-gun. They were approaching along the opposite sidewalk. A few more moments and his intended victim would be a clear target. And now, so intent was he on following her approach, he failed to see the lawman emerge from the town hall and descend the steps. Grant Symes had seen Sheba quit the hall with Trottie and wasn't about to pass up a chance to offer his help. From the bottom of the steps, he hurried after the women.

This was to be the good-looking deputy's unlucky night. Rushford had Sheba in his sights and was squeezing trigger in the instant that Symes reached the women and obscured his target.

"Can I help . . . ?"

The gunshot echoed along Main even as Symes began his offer. Trottie screamed and collapsed as Sheba loosed a gasp of pain and reeled from the deputy's sudden weight. Symes was unconscious and slumping against her when Rushford hammered back for a second shot, but now one of the Texans was reacting. Larry's Colt cleared leather as he glimpsed the gunfilled hand thrust from the alleymouth. He triggered three fast ones and, with lead whining past him, thudding into the corner at his left, Rushford cursed bitterly, whirled and made for the alley's rear end.

"Take everybody home, Dab," growled Larry. "We'll catch up later."

Stretch, already mounted, heeled his

pinto to movement. After urging him to stay after the shooter, Larry re-tied his animal and began a dash for the opposite sidewalk. He moved faster than Toddy Allsop, who overbalanced in his haste to descend the town hall steps. While Toddy fell and rolled, his boss advanced from the downtown area, panting heavily; nowadays, Phil Tarren was carrying too much blubber for swift movement.

First to reach the prone trio, Larry spared only a brief glance for the befuddled Trottie and the shocked Sheba. Blood trickled from her left upper arm, but the blonde woman was well and truly conscious. She had forgotten Trottie and was concerned only for her stricken admirer.

As he turned his matched bays, Hammond grimaced irritably.

"We're not lingering for the aftermath of this incident," he muttered.

"All that shooting . . . " murmured Anna.

"Some trigger-happy idiot," scowled

Hammond. "I don't want you involved, Sis. If we hang around, Tarren's apt to claim us as witnesses."

"Which of course we aren't," said Dortweil. "So, by all means, let's take Anna home. Distressing experience for you, my dear. Are you quite all right?"

"Just a little startled," she frowned. "And tired."

The Diamond H surrey began moving to Loomis's northern outskirts by way of Main. Though just as eager to get going, Dab gave the other surrey and its escort of soreheaded riders a fair start before following.

When Tarren and Toddy arrived, the women were on their feet and Larry kneeling by the still unconscious Symes, warily inspecting his wound.

"Somebody better start explainin' . . . " began the bosslawman.

"Oh, hell!" gasped Toddy. "It's Grant!"

"Save your damn questions," Larry growled at Tarren. "My sidekick's huntin' the skunk that gunned this

203

hombre. Anything else you want to know, it better wait till we've found a doc. And we better do that mighty pronto."

"We're almost to Alliance Road," offered Toddy. "So the new doc'd be closest."

"So what're we waitin' for?" challenged Larry. "Lend a hand here, Toddy."

"Go on home," Sheba ordered Trottie. "Don't argue, honey. Just scat. I'm goin' along with Grant."

Stretch had reached the rear end of the side alley in time to spot the fleeing drygulcher some distance north along the wider alley paralleling Main on this side. This was his man, he assured himself. He saw Rushford holster his pistol and swing astride a distinctive pony, a clean-limbed strawberry roan with white socks. To charge up the alley now might not be healthy. Plenty of lighted windows to either side suggested quite a few locals were awake. If he rushed his man now, they would sure as hell trade shots and, if the fugitive's aim was wild, some poor sonofagun could suffer the impact of a ricochet slug.

"Larry said stay after him," he recalled. "So I better get to bird-doggin' this jasper."

When Rushford hustled his mount north along the alley, the taller Texan followed, but warily, at a respectful distance.

* * *

Dr Oliver Jansen rallied quickly from the shock of being descended upon by a burly stranger, two lawmen and as many casualties. In the surgery, Sheba Gilliam insisted her wound was of little importance and begged him do his utmost for her admirer, deposited now on the white-covered table by Larry. The medico made a cursory inspection of her wound and agreed the more critical case should be treated first. In response to Larry's offer of help, he invited him to help himself to a suitable bowl, a bottle of antiseptic and everything else required for the swabbing and dressing of Sheba's wound.

"What I want to know is . . . " began Tarren.

"Let's give the doc room to work," urged Larry. "We can talk while I'm doctorin' the lady." Having collected his needs, he took the woman's good arm and asked Jansen, "Okay if we use your kitchen?"

"I'd appreciate it," said Jansen. "Less distraction if I'm left alone with this patient."

Seated in a kitchen chair, submitting to Larry's ministrations, Sheba pulled herself together and answered the sheriff's questions tersely, impatiently.

"What's to tell anyway? I was takin' Trottie home and Grant came along to help and, just as he reached us, some lowdown jasper shot him. Plain enough what happened, isn't it? The bullet went right through poor Grant and nicked me. Then this big feller and his buddy got into the action." She smiled up at Larry. "Tell 'em, Tex."

"Not much to tell," shrugged Larry.

"Is everybody gonna keep sayin' that?" grouched Tarren. "Damn it, somebody's got to know *somethin'*."

"I spotted his gunhand and got off a couple shots to faze him," offered Larry. He had swabbed the bullet-gash and was about to apply balm and fashion a dressing. "Then my partner headed for the alley. My hunch is the bush-whacker's horse was waitin' around back somewheres. So now he's on the run."

"Toddy, you go saddle up and get after 'em," ordered Tarren.

"What use?" frowned Toddy. "We don't know whichaway they headed."

"My partner'll maybe get close enough to look him over," said Larry. "That's if he don't nail him."

"I haven't deputed you or your buddy," protested Tarren. "One of my deputies has been shot and, by-Godfrey, *I'm* in charge of this investigation."

"It's all yours and welcome," Larry said offhandedly. "But Toddy couldn't do any better'n Stretch. Don't fret yourself, Sheriff. Anything my partner finds out, we'll let you know."

"A damn good deputy who deals square with everybody," scowled Tarren. "I got a big question in my mind and I'll have no peace till I find an answer."

"And the question is," said Toddy, "who'd want to kill Grant?"

"If I get my hands on the louse that gunned Grant, I'll claw his eyes out," vowed Sheba. She sighed heavily and bowed her head. "And, if Grant dies, I'm never gonna feel the same again."

"You start askin' around," Tarren urged Toddy. "Maybe somebody saw this sharpshooter. Even if you can't get a name, you can maybe get a description. Go on now. I'll hang around the surgery till the doc can tell me if Grant's got a chance."

With the kitchen to themselves,

Larry and the blonde woman traded appraisals.

"Near finished," he told her. "Just have to plaster this wad on. How're you feelin', ma'am?"

"It hurts," she shrugged. "But I'm the lucky one." Again she appraised him. "In eight years, you haven't changed any."

"I should know you from someplace?" he asked.

"The place, Larry Valentine, was Miller Gulch, Wyomin'," she said softly. "We never met, but I had my eye on you and your buddy all the time you were there, all the time you were playin' detective. Well, I guess you don't remember. And don't call me ma'am. I'm Sheba to men I like."

"We've been so many places, the beanpole and me, it's hard for us to recall names."

"The Miller Gulch law would've hung the wrong man for back-shootin' a bank cashier," said Sheba, "if you hadn't kept nosin' round till you

209

flushed out the real killer. I know how smart you are, Larry. That's why I'm gonna tell you somethin' I haven't told the sheriff. Give me a choice and I'd as soon you handled it anyway. You sure get results, don't you?"

"I get lucky is all," he said guardedly. "And not every time, Sheba." He retreated to another chair. "All finished."

"Thanks," she smiled. "Well? You want to hear about it?"

"Sheba, if you got a notion who shot that deputy, it's the sheriff you ought to be tellin'," he assured her.

"You heard me tell Phil Tarren all I know about the shootin'," she said. "This is somethin' else."

"Well . . . " he shrugged.

"I got gypped in a Missouri town — Belvort," she confided. "That was near a couple years ago. There was this good-lookin', smooth-tongued bunko man sellin' fake share certificates in the Saint Louis and Western Railroad, and guess who fell for his line? That sharper took me for twenty-five hundred. You're not interested yet? Wait till you hear this. I spotted that same cheater tonight."

"So he's here in Loomis," nodded Larry. "And that's a good reason for turnin' him in to the sheriff."

"His kind never changes," she said bitterly. "Jefferson Orwell he called himself. I'm not sure what name he goes by now, but how do you like *this*? I've heard talk of little Anna, Kyle Hammond's sister, gettin' courted in Omaha by a handsome dude and bringin' him home to Loomis to meet big brother. He's their house guest."

"So?" prodded Larry.

"So this dude could be the same Orwell," she declared. "I saw him playin' the high-toned gent out front of the town hall after the ball, handin' the Hammond girl into Kyle's surrey. You like that? Poor frail little lady like Anna Hammond gettin' the Don Juan treatment from a two-bit bunko artist. Make your blood boil, Larry?"

He was rolling a cigarette until that

moment. Now he froze, squinting at his half-built quirley, the germ of an idea forming in his mind.

"You remember Orwell good," he said quietly. "And you were there in the town hall. He likely saw you."

"Likely did," she frowned.

"If you remember him so good, why wouldn't *he* remember *you*?" he challenged.

"Hold on now," she protested. "You mean . . . ?"

"I mean you're trouble for him," said Larry. "You're the lady could warn Hammond his guest is a bunko man. So maybe this Orwell decided to shut your mouth — permanent."

"Are you sayin' . . . ?" She readjusted her bloodstained gown and gaped up at him. "No, that can't be. It couldn't have been Orwell did that shootin'."

"Didn't have to be," countered Larry. "Could've been some hombre in cahoots with him. Don't seem like it was Symes they needed to kill, does it? The way it looks to me, Symes caught up with you at a bad moment. And now that sharp-shooter's on the run, not knowin' if you're dead or alive."

"They might — try again!" she breathed. "But you won't let 'em, right? You'll give me protection?"

"Best way I can protect you is to nail the hero who tried to kill you," said Larry. "I'll do my damnedest, but I can't hunt him and sit guard on you at the same time. So you need a safe roost, Sheba." He grinned encouragingly. "And I know just the place."

"I've never been so scared in my whole life," she declared. "Just tell me what to do, Larry."

He told her what she should do, confining his advice to just a few terse sentences. And now Sheba Gilliam proved herself a reliable ally, one of his kind in fact. By the time Tarren returned to the kitchen, she was committed to Larry's strategy.

"The young doc says Grant's gonna make it," Tarren reported. "Slug didn't damage vital organs, he says. Toddy and me helped bed him down here. Be quite a time before Grant's back on his feet, but . . . "

"I'm thankful he won't die!" exclaimed Sheba. "All my fault, Phil! I'm to blame!" She rose and, to Tarren's consternation, grasped the front of his jacket and hung on like grim death. "It was *me* he was aimin' at — that killer! Poor Grant got in the way and . . . "

"You know who fired that shot?" frowned Tarren.

"Could've been any one of a dozen sore losers!" she cried. "Men I turned down! Maybe all of 'em. They got together and hired 'emselves a professional gun to kill me — couldn't stand to let any other man have me!"

"You're tearin' my jacket!" gasped Tarren. "What the hell, Sheba? You out of your mind?" Over her head, he glanced at Larry, who grimaced, raised a finger to his temple and nodded significantly. Tarren's blood ran cold. "Hell's bells!"

"I want to be locked up!" cried Sheba. "You gotta do it, Phil. Put me in a cell where they can't get at me!"

"Damn it, I can't . . . !" began Tarren.

"She'll feel safer in jail," opined Larry. "Better do like she says. After a while, she'll get to feelin' easier of mind."

The blonde woman could be very persuasive and Tarren easily intimidated. Convinced by Larry he was performing an act of charity, providing Sheba's best chance of dodging a nervous breakdown, he walked her from Alliance Road to the county jail with the even more intimidated Toddy in close attendance. Larry then returned to his horse, got mounted and started north.

Later, when he caught sight of the Circle 6 surrey and escort, he also spotted his partner. The moonlight seemed unnaturally bright tonight. From the brush bordering the trail, Stretch emerged to await him, deliberately dawdling to ensure the Freckers and their hands stayed out of earshot. Larry drew level and, stirrup-to-stirrup, they traded information.

"Right handy, all this brush," the taller Texan remarked.

"That mean he never caught on you were taggin' him?" demanded Larry.

"That's what it means," drawled Stretch. "And, before he made it to the trail and joined up with the Diamond H bunch, I got a clear look at him."

"Joined up with Hammond's bunch, huh?"

"He's one of 'em sure enough. Name's Ed Somethin'-or-other. I was just kind of loafin' along other side of the brush, listenin' good. Somebody said 'howdy, Ed.' Figured I oughtn't get greedy, so I spelled my critter, let Diamond H keep movin' and waited for our bunch to catch up."

"So a Hammond man did it."

"No mistake, runt. He rode a critter I'd know anyplace, right purty strawberry roan with white socks."

"And you'd know him anyplace?"

"Count on it. Big hombre. Real hefty. Flat-nosed. Yeah, I'll know him when I see him again. Well?" Stretch eyed Larry sidelong. "I did okay?"

"Better'n okay," said Larry. "And now I got a question, but you can't answer it and neither can I — yet."

"What question?" demanded Stretch.

"Does Hammond know one of his men put a bullet through a deputy and near-killed a woman?"

"It mightn't be Hammond's idea?" prodded Stretch.

"I aim to be mighty sure," declared Larry, "before I throw any words at Hammond. Got a hunch this Ed was followin' another man's orders."

"Sounds like you know somethin' I don't know," said Stretch.

"Enough to make me leery," confided Larry. "Somethin' stinks at Diamond H. I'm gonna tell you what I found out tonight, but we'll keep it to ourselves, savvy? It's a mite early for dealin' Dab into it."

At about the same time Larry was recounting his conversation with Sheba Gilliam to his partner, the Diamond H surrey and its escort of bruised and battered riders were crossing home range. In the rear of the vehicle, Anna and Dortweil quietly discussed the social, Hammond throwing in a remark or two until his attention was distracted by the glow of a fire a fair distance to the northeast. In response to his summons, Rushford grimaced irritably and began urging his mount up level with the driver's seat.

With plenty on his mind, no chance of talking with his co-conspirator, no way of knowing if the hapless Grant Symes were dead or alive, the rogue-ramrod kept his patience tight-reined when questioned by the rancher.

"Fire? What fire? Oh — that? Our nighthawks, I'd reckon."

"Ed, we're having another hot night. They didn't start that fire to warm themselves."

218

"No, they wouldn't do that. More likely — well — you gave the order, don't forget."

"Damn and blast."

"Any of our stock dies, we burn the carcasses."

Out of deference to his sister and their guest, Hammond dropped his voice.

"Not already. Hell, *no!*"

"There'll be rain soon enough," shrugged Rushford.

"There'll be rain," nodded Hammond. "But maybe not soon enough. Listen, I have to make sure about this. Climb up here, Ed, and take Anna and Mister Dortweil home. I'm taking your horse and riding over there." He called to his sister. "See you and Howard at breakfast. Something I have to check on."

His evening clothes were dust-smeared when, some time later, he reached the hollow where the two nighthawks tended the fire. He knew them well, Karsch and Tyree. Men who had worked for him 10 years or more.

"We won't let it spread," one of them assured him, as he reined up. "Don't worry, Mister Hammond. With the land so dry, we're doin' it real careful."

Bedeviled by the stench of the burning carcasses, Hammond grimly demanded,

"How many? I can't count them under all that timber."

"Only three head," said the other hand, long-jawed Jerry Karsch.

"*Only* three, you say?" Hammond cursed softly. "Three too many, Jerry."

The scrawny Slim Tyree said his piece.

"We had to drag 'em here from the waterhole by the old line-shack. It's all dried out, Boss. That's where they flopped. They were dead when we got to 'em."

"So it's begun," sighed Hammond.

"Mightn't be many more," Tyree half-heartedly offered. "It could rain any time."

"Before the rain comes, the whole herd could be wiped out — and you know it," growled Hammond.

"It's bad," nodded Tyree. "Still and all — what can we do but wait — and hope?"

"I'm through waiting," muttered Hammond. "There's still a way, still something I can do. And I'll do it tomorrow — early."

He confided his intentions to his sister and their guest over breakfast. Though he had plenty on his mind, plenty to worry about, he did not fail to notice Anna was accounting for a full-sized serving of ham, eggs and hot biscuits.

"Diamond H is starting to lose stock," he announced.

"Rustlers?" frowned Dortweil. "I've heard of them, but didn't imagine you had that kind of problem here."

"Not rustlers," said Hammond. "Thirst and starvation. Not water enough to keep feed grass growing. The only solution is Sun Basin."

"Kyle, you couldn't . . . " began Anna.

"Don't concern yourself, Sis," he countered. "I'm not about to trigger a range-war. Right after breakfast, I'm riding to Circle 6 to talk to Dab Frecker. I'll have cattle watering in his basin if I have to offer Frecker more money than I can afford — if I have to go down on my knees to him."

"You may well have to do that," warned Dortweil. "I'm told there was a serious flare-up during last night's social function — a less than sociable occurrence behind the town hall."

"Howard, do you think I'm ignorant of that hullabaloo?" challenged Hammond. "I know about it. I also know quite a few of my men took a beating. Apparently Frecker's men showed some spirit. Well . . . " He sighed heavily, "they can afford to. They're not watching Circle 6 stock dying of thirst."

"I suppose — you'll be safe enough," frowned Anna.

"Frecker's a stubborn old jasper, but a gentleman at heart," said Hammond. "As for his hired hands, they aren't the kind to turn trigger-happy. Anyway, I'll be visiting Frecker alone and unarmed — as a gesture of good faith."

"Will this action be approved by your own men?" asked Dortweil.

Hammond set his coffee cup down and eyed him blankly.

"Not up to them to approve or disapprove," he shrugged. "Diamond H is not a co-operative, Howard. There's only one boss, and you're looking at him."

"I'm sure you know best, Kyle," said Anna. "And it comforts me, this decision of yours. You know how I feel about the Frecker family. I've always regarded them as good neighbors. If, by making peace with Mister Frecker, you can put an end to all this enmity, I'll be proud of you."

"You — uh — seem to have quite an appetite this morning," he observed.

"That's something we can discuss

later," she smiled.

"Sure," he nodded. "When I get back from Circle 6."

Within a few minutes of Hammond's departure, Dortweil was in close conference with Rushford. The facade of serenity so admired by unsuspecting Anna was dropped in Rushford's presence; his apprehension was showing.

"Everything's going wrong," he bitterly complained. "I don't know whether or not you really silenced the Gilliam woman — that vindictive bitch — and now . . . "

"I don't know either," retorted Rushford. "One of Tarren's deputies happened along just as I triggered at her. I'm gonna have to send Burt into town in a little while. Meantime, I got no way of knowin'."

"Our situation is worse than you realize," warned Dortweil. "Hammond is desperate, but not for a war. He's on his way to Circle 6 right now — to plead with Frecker."

"Hell!" breathed Rushford.

"To come to terms with Frecker," muttered Dortweil. Rushford swore explosively as the bunko man enlarged on Hammond's intentions. "So that's what we're up against, Ed. If Diamond H and Circle 6 make peace, where do *we* stand? Who do we set up for Hammond's death?"

"If we got witnesses enough, we can still lay it at Frecker's door," insisted Rushford. "Even if him and Hammond bury the hatchet, there's still Frecker's crew. They locked horns with Diamond H men last night. They'll still be mad, savvy? So why wouldn't one of 'em tag Hammond out of Sun Basin and put a bullet in his back?"

"Well, if you think the time is ripe . . . " frowned Dortweil.

"We have to handle it this mornin'," declared Rushford. "And you have to come along. I'll need you — for bait."

Fat Pat and Elroy, making an early start at hunting bunch-quitters on the east slope, were first to sight the lone rider advancing from the direction of Diamond H.

"Great day in the mornin'!" gasped the pudgy cowpoke. "It's Kyle Hammond himself!"

8

Murder-Plan

THE other Circle 6 hand hastily joined his buddy at the basin-rim and squinted toward the approaching horseman, Kyle Hammond undoubtedly, well-mounted, rigged in expensive riding clothes. As he drew closer, the Diamond H boss raised a hand and announced,

"I'm unarmed."

"Durned if you ain't," observed Fat Pat. "Well — what . . . ?"

"Here to talk to your boss," said Hammond. "Don't worry. There'll be no trouble. All right if I ride on down to the house?"

"I guess," shrugged Fat Pat.

The arrival of the Diamond H boss caused the predictable stir. Roscoe positioned himself in the doorway of

227

his cookshack, not showing his shotgun, but keeping it within reach. Orv and Shorty emerged from the bunkhouse while, on the ranch-house porch, Dab rose from a caneback, called to his womenfolk to stay inside and advanced to the railing. Perched side by side on the toprail of the corral housing the now-malleable Whitey, the Texans puffed on thinly-rolled cigarettes and stayed impassive.

Riding into the yard, Hammond nodded to the older cattleman and voiced his request.

"Can we talk?"

"Don't see why not," shrugged Dab. "Cool your saddle, tie your mount and come join me up here. Might's well be comfortable."

He returned to his chair, filled and lit his pipe and waited patiently. Hammond climbed up to take the adjoining chair and, scorning preamble, got straight to the point.

"Found my nighthawks burning three steers last night. You know

228

what that means."

"Damn right," sighed Dab. "Beginnin' of the end. So I guess — uh . . . "

"This is a request, not a demand," said Hammond. "My back's to the wall, Frecker, so I've no choice but to . . . "

"Yeah, well, the way I see it . . . " began Dab.

"Let me finish," frowned Hammond. "Name your price. This time, I'm not trying to buy you out. I'm desperate, ready to deal. If you'll agree to allow Diamond H stock to water and graze in Sun Basin — in relays of course and strictly supervised — I'll do my damnedest to pay whatever fee you demand."

"I don't think I . . . " Dab tried again, but Hammond kept talking.

"I'm prepared to offer guarantees. The next Diamond H man tries any rough stuff with a Circle 6 hand, I'll fire him. There'll be no more harassment, Frecker. Yes, I know what you're thinking."

"I don't reckon you do."

"You're thinking your boys gave a good account of themselves last night. In that fracas behind the hall, they were outnumbered — and still they won. I'm not griping about that, Frecker. A good licking was maybe what my crew deserved. I blame myself anyway. Right from the start I resorted to bullying tactics, tried to throw my weight around. I hope you'll accept my apology for that."

"Do I get to talk now?" asked Dab. "Or ain't you finished?"

"Go ahead," offered Hammond.

"Won't be no grazin' fee," Dab said gruffly. "Have your herders start runnin' your stock into the basin rightaway, hundred head at a time. You got plenty herders, so it can be done without no trouble. With my boys keepin' Circle 6 critters yonder of the creek, up by the spring, I don't reckon we'll be mixin' brands. Part of your bunch can water at the creek, the rest of 'em by the lake. You give each bunch time enough to water and feed, then run 'em back to home range and drive another hundred in. I figure that's the best way we can handle it."

"No — grazing fee?" frowned Hammond. "You're humbling me. I don't want to be obligated."

"This is what I'd have said at the start, if you'd let me get a word in edgewise," said Dab. "Only reason I turned stubborn was you tryin' to boss me around when your water started quittin' on you. If you'd asked then, as one neighbor to another, we'd never have tangled. 'Stead of askin', you had to act proddy. All right, you up and apologized. Takes a real man to admit he's done wrong. Fine. I respect you for that and we'll not talk of it again. You don't have to feel humble nor obligated. It's just, if I took money from you, I'd feel like I was profitin' from your misfortune. I ain't about to do that, so let's not argue about it."

Hammond bowed his head — after shaking it dazedly.

"I've been too damn arrogant," he accused himself. "Right from the start, Frecker. No patience. No goodwill."

"You had plenty to fret about," said Dab. "Too much frettin' can sour a man's disposition. Now, how soon d'you want to set this up?"

"I'll take till tomorrow morning to get it all organized," said Hammond. "Let's say I'll have my hands drive the first hundred in around mid-morning. Okay by you?"

"Fine," nodded Dab. "Anything else? I could have Addy fix you some coffee."

"Thanks, and my respects to Mrs Frecker, but I'd better be getting back," said Hammond. He rose and offered his hand. "I'll remember you for this, old timer. God forbid you should ever see your herd failing. But, if that day ever comes, I'll treat you as you've treated me. Diamond H will help out."

"Man can't ask for more from a neighbor," said Dab, rising to shake hands.

A sadder, wiser and much relieved Kyle Hammond thanked him again, descended from the porch and untied his horse. By then, to the surprise of all, the Texans were leading their saddled mounts out of the barn.

"Fat Pat and Elroy don't need no help," Orv called to them as they swung astride.

"We'll be back in a little while, Orv," Larry promised. "These cayuses could use some exercise."

"Over here, Orv." Dab beckoned his foreman. "Got things to tell you."

A few minutes after quitting the basin, the Diamond H boss threw a glance over his shoulder. The tall riders were moving clear of the rim, headed his way. His curiosity aroused, he slowed his pace.

"This couldn't be Frecker's idea," he opined, as they came up on either side of him. "I guess you don't know it yet. We've settled our differences, so there'll be no more trouble between Diamond H and Circle 6."

"Glad to hear that," drawled Larry.

"Me too," nodded Stretch. "We like for everything to stay peaceable, Mister Hammond."

"You have the advantage of me," frowned Hammond.

"He's Valentine, I'm Emerson," offered Stretch.

"You and Dab talked turkey, huh?" prodded Larry.

"Your boss is giving me a chance to save my herd," said Hammond. "I have his permission to water Diamond H stock in the basin."

"Sounds fine," said Larry. "But you still got trouble."

Hammond frowned again.

"Just what are you talking about, Valentine?"

"Feller name of Ed rides for you," said Larry. "You know who I mean?"

"Only one man of that name on my payroll," said Hammond. "My foreman. Ed Rushford."

"Would he be a heavyset hombre, flat-nosed?" asked Stretch. "Favors a right handsome saddle-animal, strawberry roan with white socks?"

"That's Ed Rushford," nodded Hammond. "What about him?"

"As I recall, you Diamond folks was about to head home last night when the shootin' started," said Larry.

"That gunplay was no concern of mine," retorted Hammond.

"Don't bet on that," countered Larry. "I got things to tell you, mister. And, unless you're ten kinds of a fool, you'll listen good and mind what I say."

They had reached Diamond H land by the time Larry was through belaboring Hammond with the harsh facts. He began by emphasizing Sheba Gilliam's positive identification of the man Hammond knew as Howard Dortweil, followed that with a brief explanation of the protective arrest of the blonde woman and added a grim assurance.

"That's how it had to be done. Outside of the county jail, her life wouldn't be worth a plugged dime. Plain enough — or are you gonna give me an argument? Dortweil, or Orwell, or whatever his name is, must've spotted her before she spotted him. But he didn't take a shot at her. The bastard behind the gun was your foreman."

"You'd better be able to prove . . . !" began Hammond.

"Talk to him," Larry urged Stretch.

Now, in his rambling way, the taller Texan told of his skilful trailing of the sniper, repeated his description and told of seeing Rushford join the homebound Diamond H group, of hearing Rushford greeted by name. By then, Hammond was tense and hard-eyed, a nerve twitching at his temple, his teeth clenched.

"Just two things you can do," muttered Larry. "Don't believe any of it. Call us a couple crazy liars."

"And — the other thing?" challenged Hammond.

"Face up to the truth," growled

Larry. "The dude courtin' your sister ain't what he claims to be. He's bad medicine for the likes of her."

"And — he and my foreman . . . ?"

"In cahoots. How about that? They been gettin' together since Dortweil came to Loomis?"

"Well, they seem to get along."

"How good d'you know this Rushford?" Hammond grimaced in disgust.

"Apparently I've been as foolish as Anna. I've trusted Rushford as readily as she trusts Dortweil." He swore softly. "It'll go hard on her. I don't know how to explain this to her." Staring hard at Larry, he declared, "I'm not sure I should. You could be playing wild hunches, Valentine."

"Still leery, huh?" prodded Larry. "We've dealt it out for you, but it's too rich for your blood — you don't want to buy it?"

"Mighty far-fetched," breathed Hammond. "And hasn't *this* occurred to you? You're meddling. None of it is any of your business."

"Listen, Hammond, I'm sorry about your sister, but I'm makin' it my business," warned Larry. "Why am I meddlin'? I want to know why they're doin' what they're doin'. Has to be a reason."

"And my ol' buddy was born curious," drawled Stretch. "He never did take kindly to a mystery, always has to find a reason for every doggone thing."

"A woman-killer on my payroll," scowled Hammond. "You expect me to believe . . . ?"

"Rushford tried to gun the Gilliam woman no matter what you say," Larry grimly assured him. "And maybe he ain't the only killer on your payroll. Last time a raidin' party hit Circle 6, they wore hoods. We fazed 'em into the brush west of the basin and they set it afire, damn near burned us alive. Now I'm askin' you — did you order that raid? Did you order any killin'?"

"Damn it, no!" protested Hammond. "Scare-raids, yes. But a murder-raid? Never."

"So, like it or not, you got five bad hombres in your bunkhouse crew," declared Larry.

Their mounts were carrying them upward now. Above and dead ahead was a timbered hogsback. Hammond was travelling a short-cut and his tall companions automatically tagging along. He fished out a kerchief and mopped at his face as he recalled,

"I hired five others when I hired Rushford. All six of them showed up at the same time."

"And now you ain't so sure about Rushford and his budies," guessed Stretch.

"They — don't bunk with the other hands," frowned Hammond. He began a protest when they reached the summit of the hogsback. "But I still can't believe . . ."

"Hold it." Larry, first to reach the north edge of the woody pine, suddenly drew rein and signaled Stretch and the rancher to follow suit. "Well, well, well."

"Now what?" demanded Stretch.

"Come take a look, but don't show yourselves," urged Larry, delving into his saddlebag. He produced his field-glasses and offered them to Hammond. "You first. Looks like a pow wow. Seven hombres cravin' privacy — and one of 'em looks like your fancy-pants friend Dortweil."

They dismounted, advanced to the outer edge and bellied down. Through the binoculars, Hammond intently studied the seven men squatting by their ground-reined horses on open ground some 50 yards from the ridge. East of the group, a stand of trees extended to and beyond the outer reaches of the ridge. After noting the group was positioned only 25 yards from those trees, the Texans traded glances. No words were necessary; they shared the same thought.

"Howard Dortweil — and Rushford," observed Hammond. "The other five are . . . "

"Same five tried to roast us, bet your boots," drawled Stretch.

"It does look like a parley," Hammond said bitterly, returning the glasses. "Dortweil and Rushford have plenty to talk about, the way it looks from here." As they retreated from the edge, he cursed luridly. "I have to know for sure! And I'd rather challenge Dortweil here — than back at the house — where Anna might get involved."

"Gonna ride right on down and brace Dortweil, huh?" asked Larry.

"And don't try to talk me out of it," growled Hammond.

"I won't," Larry assured him. "Only give us time enough to make it to the timber east of where they're squattin'."

"Don't worry," soothed Stretch. "We'll go down quiet. And, when you say your piece, we'll be coverin' you."

Hammond gaped at them.

"What the hell're you talking about? I'll be in no danger."

"Just in case," shrugged Larry. "And — uh — don't look to the trees, savvy? Just keep your eyes on Dortweil and them hard cases. You can forget about

241

us — 'less we get the idea we ought to buy in."

Seething with impatience, Hammond waited a full 5 minutes after the Texans had remounted to ride to the east end of the ridge. From there, with the trees screening their movements, they worked their way into the timber, cooled their saddles, secured their animals and stared westward, ears cocked to the hoofbeats of the rancher's animal; Hammond had descended and was hustling his mount toward Dortweil and Company. Larry slid his Winchester from its scabbard levered a shell into the breech and enquired,

"You ready?"

"Uh huh," grunted Stretch, drawing his matched .45's. "So here we go again."

The seven rose to their feet to frown at the grim-faced rider reining up beside their animals. As Hammond swung down, Dortweil summoned up an urbane grin.

"Hello there, Kyle my friend. Didn't

expect to see you out here."

"I'll bet," Hammond said bitterly, moving toward him. "Tell me something!" He confronted Dortweil, glaring into his face, ignoring the other men. "What's the *real* name? Dortweil — or Jefferson Orwell?"

Dortweil's jaw sagged.

"Kyle, I haven't the slightest idea what you . . . "

"What makes you think Mister Dortweil is somebody else?" demanded Rushford.

"Interested, are you?" Hammond challenged him. "You *would* be, wouldn't you? Some bungler you are, Rushford. I'm pretty sure it was you tried to silence the Gilliam woman — with a bullet — and you and Dortweil know *why*." He glowered at Dortweil again. "I've already talked to her." The lie came easily; despite his emotional state, he was capable of cunning in a tight situation. "She has blackmail on her mind, so she hasn't talked to anybody else, refuses to testify against you unless

I make it worth her trouble. I won't do that, so now what? Will you pay for her silence?"

Dortweil studied him a long moment, then shrugged and remarked to Rushford, "I don't think we'll do it that way, Ed."

"Better to shut her mouth," muttered Rushford, as he drew his Colt. Simultaneously, Burt Marcus grinned an ugly grin and filled his hand. "Only safe way, only way to be sure of her. As for Hammond, do I need to say it?"

"Obviously, this has to be the time," drawled Dortweil.

Hammond backstepped a pace. The Smith and Wesson had appeared quickly and he was taken by surprise, had never suspected Dortweil's well-tailored coat concealed a shoulder-holster. His scalp crawled. He was wondering how much support he could expect from the Texans when he coldly challenged Dortweil.

"Why? Tell me why! I've a right to know!"

"Let *me* tell him," grinned Rushford. "I'm gonna enjoy this!"

"So enjoy yourself, but quickly," urged Dortweil. "I want to get this over and done with."

"You're a dead man, Mister High-And-Mighty Hammond," jeered Rushford. "That slow-brained sister of yours'll mourn you quite a time. Oh, sure. She'll need comfortin' — from my partner here."

"Anna will come to rely on me, Hammond," smiled Dortweil. "After a decent period has passed, we'll be married of course. She'll inherit Diamond H and, as her husband, I'll damn soon take control."

"So that's what's behind it all?" raged Hammond. "Diamond H — run by a partnership of thieves!"

"Drought can't last forever, Hammond," said Rushford.

"A rich prize, Diamond H," declared Dortweil.

"And we've planned everything good," bragged Rushford. "It'll be some dumb

245

Circle 6 waddy hangs for your murder."

"We'll all be witnesses," chuckled Marcus.

"Dortweil — or whatever your name is . . . " snarled Hammond, "you're a lowdown sonofabitch!"

To the surprise of the conspirators, also the watching Texans, he dared three leveled guns by rushing at Dortweil and seizing his right wrist. Rushford and Marcus promptly began maneuvering for a clear shot at the rancher and the other men dropped hands to holsters while, bounding out of the timber, the Texans announced themselves, Larry with a bellowed demand, Stretch with an ear-piercing rebel yell.

"Drop the hardware!"

Challenged by only two men, the hard cases whirled to open fire and, at that moment, Hammond shoved Dortweil off-balance while still clinging to him. They went down heavily, struggling for possession of the S & W. A fast-triggered slug came low at the taller Texan, actually searing the leather of his pants-belt at the left side. His Colts boomed and wreaked havoc, his righthand weapon accounting for Rushford, his other smashing a gunarm, putting a hard case down to writhe in agony.

Two slugs whined dangerously close to Larry as he made his play. The Winchester was discharged with its stock jammed into his left hip and the muzzle directed unerringly at Marcus, who hurtled backward with his Colt discharging to the sky and his chest red-stained. Then Larry's .45 was out and booming and another man lurching from the impact of the bullet smashing his collarbone.

Face to face, locked together, Hammond and Dortweil still pitted their strength against each other. The rancher saw death in Dortweil's derisive eyes as, with a last mighty effort, he hauled upward on Dortweil's wrist and twisted savagely. In the instant before it discharged, the pistol's muzzle was an inch from Dortweil's ribs; his anguished cry merged with the report and, as his body became limp, Hammond wrenched the weapon free, re-cocked it and rolled over to check the scene of conflict. He was still being deafened by the roar of Colts, anticipating he would have to take a hand, when the battle abruptly ended.

Stretch was prone and bleeding from a thigh-wound, Larry crouched on one knee, when their Colts boomed for the last time. Larry's victim went down with his head bloody. Stretch's target dropped his smoking weapon, clasped both hands to his right side and, groaning, flopped on his backside.

As the echoes of those gunshots died away, Larry proved he was unscathed by regaining his feet.

"How bad?" he growled to his partner.

"Don't reckon I'm totin' a bullet," mumbled Stretch. "But that slug sure tore a chunk outa my leg. Gonna feel a heap better when it quits leakin' blood."

"Hammond . . . ?" called Larry.

"Dortweil is dead," Hammond said harshly. "And I never felt better!"

"Collect guns." Larry made it an order, not a request. "I'll do what I can for the beanpole's leg while you load them dead heroes onto their horses."

"Only place for the survivors is the county jail," scowled Hammond.

"Ain't that the truth," mumbled Stretch. "With them polecats in the pokey, the air around Diamond H is gonna smell some cleaner."

Returning from where they had left their horses a short time later, Larry uncorked a bottle of whiskey and hunkered beside his partner.

"Sorry, big feller," he gently apologized. "This is gonna hurt."

"Funny," sighed Stretch. "I just knew you were gonna say that."

Having doctored the wounded hard cases as best he could, Hammond made short work of lashing the dead men to horses. He then hurried across to where Larry worked on his partner, fashioning a makeshift dressing for his ugly wound.

"I'll postpone my speech of gratitude, Valentine," he muttered. "This isn't the time for it."

"Damn right," agreed Larry.

"Naturally I'll help deliver the wounded to the sheriff," said Hammond. "After that . . . " He shook his head worriedly, "it will be my miserable duty to explain everything to my sister, a lady who deserves better."

"Rough," grunted Larry.

"But, before I ride home, I'll have quite a statement to offer the sheriff," said Hammond. "One of those wounded men did a lot of talking before losing consciousness, probably imagining his last moment was at hand."

"Somethin' interestin', huh?" prodded Larry.

"They were outlaws, Rushford and his buddies," said Hammond. "Fled Kansas with a posse hounding them. Dortweil was a bunko man sure enough and a close cohort of Rushford. I was being set up, Valentine. They meant to kill me and let some Circle 6 man be charged on their perjured evidence. Then Dortweil would have married Anna — after she inherited the ranch."

"So Dortweil and Rushford and their dirty sidekicks would've owned the richest spread in the territory," mused Larry. He secured the dressing and, while feeding his partner a stiff shot of whiskey, casually remarked, "I'm glad you told me. Like the beanpole said, I don't like mysteries, like to know what's behind it all."

"That kind of curiosity must be dangerous sometimes," opined Hammond.

"What d'you mean — sometimes?" grimaced Larry. "*All* the time."

★ ★ ★

It was Sheriff Phil Tarren's proud boast that he never drank while on duty. This was to be the day he would have to give up on that boast because, when

251

he saw the grim procession advancing toward his office, Larry helping Stretch stay astride the pinto, Kyle Hammond herding the animals toting the dead and wounded, he felt a sudden need of fortification and acted accordingly, retreating into his office to partake of a generous slug from his private liquor supply.

Moving out of Alliance Road after paying a courtesy call on the slowly-recovering Deputy Symes, Toddy Allsop gaped at the Diamond H boss, then at the Texans, then made a beeline for the law office. As he arrived, his boss came out onto the porch.

"All right, Toddy, all right. I see 'em."

"What's *happenin'* to Loomis County?" wondered Toddy. "Grant shot last night and Miss Sheba near killed — and now *this*!"

"Those Texans again," Tarren said sternly.

"Yeah, but Mister Hammond too," frowned Toddy.

"Fetch Doc Conrad," ordered Tarren. "Not all those horses are totin' dead men."

Having advanced close enough to overhear the sheriff's command, Hammond called to him.

"You'll be taking the wounded into custody, Sheriff Tarren. A charge of attempted murder. Better send for a J.P. as well."

"Whatever you say, Mister Hammond," nodded Tarren.

"Have somebody take these stiffs to the undertaker," urged Larry, as he began turning his and Stretch's animals. "I'm gonna leave Hammond to do all the talkin'."

"I'll want statements . . . !" began Tarren.

"If that other doc's home, that's where you'll find us," Larry called over his shoulder. "I want it to be him patches my partner."

"I'll settle for the barber — a saloon-gal if she's purty — a horse-doctor — anybody at all . . . "

253

mumbled Stretch.

"Now, see here . . . !" blustered Tarren.

"And you can turn Sheba loose now," Larry added as an afterthought. "If she's got the stomach for it, she can identify one of them stiffs and tell you quite a story."

An hour passed before Hammond could break loose from the sheriff and head back to Diamond H to break the bad news to his sister. He was anxious to get that sorry chore over and done with, but also mindful of his debt to the Texans. So, from the law office, he made his way to the home of Dr Oliver Jansen.

The medico greeted him diffidently and conducted him to a room containing two cots. Grant Symes occupied one. Stretch, ignoring Jansen's protests, was rising from the other, insisting on trying his feet.

"Quit your frettin', Doc," he chided. "You patched my leg real slick. I'll rest it, sure, but in my bunk at Circle 6. No offense to Deputy Symes here. It's just I'd feel plumb peculiar with a lawman for a room-mate."

"Doc got curious, asked a whole lot of questions," Larry remarked to Hammond.

"And you told him — everything?" frowned Hammond.

"You objectin'?" challenged Larry. "Listen, everybody'd hear of it anyway. It couldn't be kept quiet."

"I guess not," shrugged Hammond. "Only stopped by to thank you and Emerson for all you've done — which certainly includes saving my life."

"You're welcome," shrugged Stretch.

"Think nothin' of it," grunted Larry, taking his partner's arm. "Here we go, stringbean. Lean on me."

"I've been — lying here — listening..." began Symes.

"Don't try to talk," ordered Jansen. "You've had a near-miraculous escape so — please — don't undo all my good work by overtaxing your strength." At that point, Sheba came bustling in to plant herself in the chair beside the deputy's cot. "Another visitor?"

"And don't tell me to leave till I'm good and ready," she warned him. "I'm here to help, Doc. Just let me sit with him. I won't even talk to him if you'd as soon I didn't."

"I believe it would be safe to leave my patient a while, and that's most fortunate," said Jansen, staring hard at Hammond. "Because I intend accompanying you, Mister Hammond."

"Now, Jansen, this is family business," Hammond pointed out. "I can do my sad duty by my sister without your professional help."

"But I'm concerned!" Jansen said impulsively.

Hammond eyed him intently.

"Professionally — or personally?"

"Both," declared Jansen.

"I think you'd better explain that," said Hammond.

"Professionally, because she may suffer severe shock," said Jansen. "Let's not forget you're about to inform her she was being wooed by a rogue, a man conspiring to murder you. I will insist, if I deem it necessary, on administering a sedative."

"And what's your personal interest?" demanded Hammond.

"Well . . ." Jansen shrugged uncomfortably. "It might be some small consolation to her — knowing she has won the admiration of — well — a man less likely to cause her distress."

"Is that so?" Hammond challenged, contemplating him. "All right, I'm ready to go. You want to rent a saddle animal?"

"If you don't mind waiting just a few more minutes, I'll harness my buggyhorse," said Jansen.

Later, while slowly riding toward Sun Basin, the trouble shooters waxed philosophical. Stretch's pain was the more intense, but Larry's ribs still ached from the battle of the town hall's rear yard; both drifters felt a mite toilworn right now.

"Proves how wrong we can be, huh?"

remarked Stretch. "Even workin' a friendly little spread like Circle 6, we still get prodded into all kinds of strife."

"The kind we couldn't ride away from," argued Larry.

"I guess so," shrugged Stretch.

"I've heard it said lightnin' don't strike twice in the same place," mused Larry. "Tell you what, amigo. We oughtn't quit yet, ought to stay on for round-up, help drive the herd to Omaha just like we promised Dab. I figure it'll be peaceful enough from here on."

"Be like old times, huh?" Stretch wistfully suggested. "Roundin' 'em up. Drivin' 'em to the railhead?"

"And near gettin' our butts full of lead fightin' somebody else's fight," sighed Larry. "That was like old times too."

"Ain't that the truth," agreed Stretch.

They were glad to see Circle 6 again. To their battle-weary eyes, the ranchhouse, barn and corrals, the bunkhouse, the cook-shack and Roscoe's still, were a pleasing sight as they made their slow descent of the south slope. On the other side of the basin, up along the slopes, Shorty, Fat Pat and Elroy kept busy flushing fractious, well-fed steers from the chaparral and down to sweet graze. The spring, the creek and the lake sparkled in the sunshine. Dab and his foreman smoked and talked over by the bunkhouse while evil odors wafted from the still.

Yes, it was good to be returning to a temporary home. By round-up time, Stretch's wound would have healed sufficiently for him to handle his share of the chores. They would stay on for the drive to Omaha but, by then, the old itch would be affecting them, the wanderlust bedeviling them.

Soon enough, the trouble-shooters would be 'on the drift' again.

Epilogue

WITHIN the year, Reverend SAM PICKARD joined several Loomis County couples in holy matrimony.

ANNA HAMMOND did suffer the predictably adverse reaction upon learning of her suitor's duplicity and treachery. But, to the great relief of her brother, KYLE HAMMOND, that period of anguish was mercifully short. She did not revert to her inadequate diet nor become an embittered recluse, thanks to the understanding and constant attention of Dr OLIVER JANSEN, whom her brother soon acknowledged as a far worthier suitor for her hand. Some months later, the young doctor's proposal was accepted by a happier, healthier Anna.

The drought was broken by good rainfalls some 6 weeks after Diamond H began relaying cattle into Sun Basin for feed and water. By late spring round-up, eighty percent of Hammond's stock was in as prime condition as DAB FRECKER's payherd. The two cattlemen, like good neighbors the West over, agreed to make it a combined drive.

After being paid off in Omaha, LARRY VALENTINE and STRETCH EMERSON resumed their aimless drifting. There was one brief celebration in Omaha, a send-off by Dab and his old hands, and then they surrendered to their wanderlust and got moving.

A few weeks after Deputy GRANT SYMES was pronounced fit by his doctor, he renounced bachelorhood in favor of wedded bliss with the only-too-willing SHEBA GILLIAM.

And still the wedding bells rang. His courage boosted by ROSCOE CULLY's first and never-to-be-repeated successful distillation, a whiskey of rare quality, SHORTY RUDGE adopted a tougher, less diffident attitude toward

Dab's younger daughter. This show of forcefulness made a profound impression on LUCY LOU FRECKER, who became Mrs Rudge a few months later.

DESDEMONA FRECKER, chagrined that Grant Symes was now wed to another, caused her parents considerable concern by marrying TODDY ALLSOP on the rebound. The morning after the wedding and from that time onward, however, the Freckers saw no cause for further concern. It was obvious to all that radiant Desdemona was over joyed by the marital state; people just had to conclude that Toddy "must be doing something right."

THE LAWMAN WORE BLACK
THE DUDE MUST DIE
WAIT FOR THE JUDGE
HOLD 'EM BACK!
WELLS FARGO DECOYS

TOP HAND
Wade Everett

The Broken T was big. But no ranch is big enough to let a man hide from himself.

GUN WOLVES OF LOBO BASIN
Lee Floren

The Feud was a blood debt. When Smoke Talbot found the outlaws who gunned down his folks he aimed to nail their hide to the barn door.

SHOTGUN SHARKEY
Marshall Grover

The westbound coach carrying the indomitable Larry and Stretch headed for a shooting showdown.